"You've been thinking about me, too." He caught her hand, held it in a relaxed grip.

"No."

His thumb whisked over knuckles. "Admit it, Sophie." She made one final albeit halfhearted attempt to pull away, but his gaze held hers and he lifted her hand to his chest. His heart thumped strong and deep. "You've been wondering about our first kiss all day," he continued in that low seductive tone. "Like when..." Still massaging the base of her scalp, he leaned in, touched warm, firm lips to hers. *Oh, my.* "And where..." Heat flowed like honey as he slid the tip of his tongue over her bottom lip. "And how..."

When not teaching or writing, **ANNE OLIVER** loves nothing more than escaping into a book. She keeps a box of tissues handy—her favorite stories are intense, passionate, against-all-odds romances. Eight years ago, she began creating her own characters in paranormal and time-travel adventures, before turning to contemporary romance. Other interests include quilting, astronomy, all things Scottish and eating anything she doesn't have to cook. Sharing her characters' journeys with readers all over the world is a privilege…and a dream come true. Anne lives in Adelaide, South Australia, and has two adult children. Visit her website at www.anne-oliver.com. She loves to hear from readers. Email her at anne@anne-oliver.com.

HER NOT-SO-SECRET DIARY

ANNE OLIVER

~ His Very Personal Assistant ~

Harlequin®

TORONTO NEW YORK LONDON
AMSTERDAM PARIS SYDNEY HAMBURG
STOCKHOLM ATHENS TOKYO MILAN MADRID
PRAGUE WARSAW BUDAPEST AUCKLAND

Recycling programs
for this product may
not exist in your area.

ISBN-13: 978-0-373-52824-0

HER NOT-SO-SECRET DIARY

First North American Publication 2011

This edition published by arrangement with Harlequin Books S.A.

For questions and comments about the quality of this book
please contact us at Customer_eCare@Harlequin.ca.

® and TM are trademarks of the publisher. Trademarks indicated with
® are registered in the United States Patent and Trademark Office, the
Canadian Trade Marks Office and in other countries.

www.Harlequin.com

Printed in U.S.A.

HER NOT-SO-SECRET DIARY

To old cats and favourite places in the sun.
Miss you, Cleo.

Thanks to Kathy, Linda, Sharon and Lynn
for your advice on all things PA, and to Meg
for her valued insight and suggestions.

CHAPTER ONE

OH…THE things the man could do… He was the most creative lover she'd ever had. She'd enjoyed a few but this one was the flame on her Flaming Sambuca. Slithering lower, Sophie Buchanan licked the lingering flavour of blackberries and cream from her lips. As sweet as it was, she was done with dessert.

The silk sheets slid cool and smooth against her skin, the perfect foil for his hard, hot weight as she arched her body beneath him. Wanting more. Wanting everything. And she told him what that was. Every glorious detail.

Then she sighed as he set about fulfilling those requests, starting at her ear lobe and working his way down.

His mouth was warm, wet and wicked, suckling at her neck, laving her collarbone and sending goose bumps from the roots of her hair right down to the tips of her toes and every throbbing place in between. His thumbs, lightly calloused, chafed her sensitised flesh as he tweaked her nipples until…oh…bliss… she was in heaven.

'There's more,' his gravel and whisky voice promised.

She hummed her approval, absorbing the scent and texture of his skin against hers while his hands continued their erotic journey.

Wanting to absorb the feel of his flesh through her fingertips, she slid her fingers slowly down his spine, touching every vertebra in turn, pressing her thumbs into the hard muscle on either side. She was rewarded with a harsh groan that tickled her ear and told her he was enjoying it as much as she.

Then he touched her some more. Everywhere. Everywhere at once. His fingers sought, found and satisfied all her secret places. Ripples of pleasure flowed through her veins like liquid gold—his expertise knew no bounds and it seemed his only desire was to bring her pleasure.

And he did, in *every* way. *Jared…* The name rippled through her mind like silken ribbons in a tropical breeze.

He smiled, traced her mouth with a finger then with his tongue, and she smiled too, before indulging in the most sumptuous of kisses. He tasted rich and dark, like the blackberries and cream they'd shared, and ever-so-slightly dangerous, which was okay, since she knew she was perfectly safe with him.

Yes… Perfection.

He kneed her thighs apart then slid inside her with agonisingly exquisite slowness. It was as if the world forgot to turn. As if it were coming to a stop. And perhaps it was. Perhaps it had ceased to exist, because it seemed it was only the two of them in a sparkling cocoon of everlasting velvet night.

And then…

She heard a moan, as if her voice came from somewhere else, and her eyes slid open, the darkness alive and glowing with wonder, the tidal wave of her climax still crashing around her. She lay a moment listening to the sound of her elevated breathing while her body slowly floated back to earth.

And reality.

She touched her still tingling lips, realised she was still smiling. And why wouldn't she be? Oh…my…goodness.

As her eyes adjusted to night's soft glow through her living-room window, she saw the Gold Coast's languid summer's evening had sprinkled the indigo sky with silver dust.

A dream. And the best sex she'd never had.

Yet even though his image remained tantalisingly vague, she could still taste him on her tongue. Which was as fanciful as it was true, she knew, but that didn't make it any less sumptuous. As dream lovers went he was a five-star keeper. Which, all things considered, was a shame because why weren't there any men out there in the real world to compare?

She shook her head against the cushion. It didn't matter if there were a zillion comparable men beating a path to her door, she wasn't interested. She didn't need—or want—a real man in her life ever again. Not after Glen. He'd destroyed what they had and left her feeling less than a woman. Her dream lovers suited her just fine. Dream lovers were all about you and your wants and they didn't let you down.

Best of all, they were safe.

Her laptop lay on the coffee table, its tiny power light winking in the dimness. Rousing herself, she switched on the reading lamp. *Every luscious detail, before the glory fades.*

Even though she no longer attended counselling sessions, the dream journal she still kept was on her night-stand, so she dragged the computer onto her lap, created a dream folder, flexed her fingers…

His name was Jared, and this dream hottie could scorch her sheets any time he wanted… The words flowed onto the screen, tantalising her all over again. She reread the document, flushing hot as she did so. *Whew*, it was like reading one of those steamy romance novels. What would her counsellor have made of it?

Then her fingers stalled above the keyboard. *Jared?* Her heart thumped once and a jolt of heat arrowed through her body. She didn't know anyone by that name… Unless she counted Jared Sanderson—and it couldn't be him. How could you have the hots for a guy you'd never met, let alone seen up close? Pam's boss. And since her friend was off work sick and Sophie was temping for her, that made him *her* boss for the next day or so.

A shivery sensation shot through her body, making the tiny hairs on the back of her neck and down her arms stand up. A glimpse of dark cropped hair and a snowy white shirt stretched tight over impossibly broad shoulders when she'd arrived at the office of J Sanderson Property Investments and Refurbishments this morning…

She shook the image away. Big boss Jared had been too busy or simply too rude to bother introducing himself to his lowly temporary PA before heading out for the rest of the day.

It wasn't *him*, she told herself firmly. The name had stuck in her mind, that was all. Not to mention that stunning physique… And tall and dark had always been her thing…

No. If he *had* hit her sweet spot on some subconscious level and it had manifested in her dreams, it didn't matter since he'd *never know.*

So it wasn't a problem. Not a problem at all. Nor was she going to allow this particular dream lover to erode the competent professional image she'd worked so hard for. She'd come to Surfers to bury past hurts, to begin a new life.

Professional. It reminded her that she'd not yet emailed the file Pam had asked her to edit before forwarding to the office. Switching to email, she entered the address Pam had supplied and began a brief accompanying note. *Dear Jared…*

She paused. Typing those words redefined the image and rekindled the smouldering heat in her lower body to life again. She fanned a hand in front of her face, a smile tugging at her mouth despite herself. Where the heck was that professionalism?

She deleted the words, then shook her fingers in front of her for a few seconds, pursed her lips and began again. *Mr Sanderson…* Much better. *Please find the Lygon and Partners report attached for your approval. Regards, Sophie Buchanan for Pam Albright.*

She attached Pam's revised document, pressed Send, then closed her computer and the lamp and headed to her bedroom through the shadows. She settled back against the pillows with a sigh. Maybe she'd get lucky some more.

She'd barely closed her eyes when something sharp and hot and possibly terminal lodged dead centre in her chest, and they snapped wide open again. She couldn't have… She *Could Not.*

Jackknifing up, she stumbled back to the living room and her laptop and stabbed the On button. Her fingers twitched with impatience while the little computer took its sweet time powering up. For heaven's sake, could it load any slower?

When her email screen appeared she scrolled to her Sent Items folder and…her breath stopped. Her heart stopped. Everything stopped. *Oh. My. God.*

Her dream file was this very minute awaiting Jared Sanderson's approval.

Her heart restarted and hysterical laughter bubbled up her throat as she quickly attached the correct document and resent. Did the man have a sense of humour? According to Pam, no, he didn't, and her mouth twisted as she blew out a breath.

Even if he did see the humour in the situation, what she'd written was so shockingly…well, shocking. The worst, the very worst of it, was his name was in there. Only his first name, but that was more than enough… She was never ever going to put her sexy dreams in writing again.

The swipe card they'd given her didn't operate the building's front door so there was no point going to the office now to try and delete it. Which meant she'd have to wait till someone opened up in the morning to get into the office. Seven o'clock at the earliest.

With a groan, she let her head fall back and gazed at the ceiling. But she didn't see it. All she saw was the look on the man's face when he opened her email.

She was so dead.

He was an uncle. Jared strolled into his living room just after 10:00 p.m. with two glasses and a bottle of the best Aussie Chardonnay. A niece. Arabella Fleur. Cute as a cupcake, with a mop of dark hair, big eyes and a rosebud mouth. Fingers and toes all accounted for. The grin he'd been wearing since Crystal had delivered her firstborn this afternoon seemed to be permanently carved into his cheeks.

His youngest sister Melissa was home already; he could hear the shower running. Setting the bottle and glasses on the coffee table, he sat on the sofa and checked his phone for messages and the day's office emails. He gave most only a cursory glance. Pam would have phoned with anything urgent.

Sophie Buchanan. The unfamiliar name popped up with a reference to the Lygon report. Ah…now he remembered Pam had gone home sick yesterday. Crystal's nine-fifteen call this morning informing him she was in labour ten days early and that Ian's flight wasn't due in from Sydney for another hour had pushed everything and everyone out of his mind. Sophie must be the temp Pam had organised.

'Hey, Liss?' he called when he heard movement in the hallway. 'Get your butt in here. We've got some celebrating to do.' He popped the cork and filled the glasses as Melissa appeared in the doorway, wrapped in her robe, her red hair damp about her face.

'Ooh, lovely.' She wasted no time padding across the room and taking the proffered glass.

'Special occasion, *Auntie* Melissa.'

She grinned, clinked her glass to his but remained standing. 'Welcome to the world, Arabella Fleur.' She sipped then said, 'She's got your ears. Nice and flat.'

He tasted the wine, then grinned back, chuffed with the idea that some tiny part of him at least was immortal. 'You think?'

'I do. This is nice.' Another sip, followed by a long, slow swallow. Her brows arched over her aquamarine eyes as she glanced at the label. 'But I still prefer the French variety.'

The bubbles fizzed on his tongue as he studied her. Their father's death had left the three of them orphans. He'd been eighteen, Crystal thirteen, Melissa just six. She'd never known their mother, who'd died when she was two weeks old. When had that little girl become this sophisticated young woman? Too sophisticated. 'You're not supposed to be experienced enough to know the difference.'

'Oh, *pul-lease*, I'm nearly eighteen.' She swung away. 'You sound like a father.'

Her accusation took the shine off. Twelve years ago Jared had taken on the role and responsibilities of both parents. And he didn't regret it for a minute. But sometimes...

'Maybe,' he acknowledged. 'But I won't apologise for it. I love you, Lissa, and that's never going to change.'

'I know.' Her voice softened and she shook her head. 'But sometimes...'

Yeah. Raising Lissa had been the most challenging experience of his life. And he had a feeling the hardest part wasn't done yet. The letting-go part.

'Speaking of fathers...and babies and all...' Twirling her glass, she pinned him with the same intense gaze. 'When are you going to find some poor girl who's willing to put up with your conservative ways and start a family of your own?' *And let me get on with my life,* her eyes said.

To avoid her familiar rant, he picked up his phone again, flicked through his messages once more. 'No hurry. I still have you to look out for.'

She made a noise at the back of her throat. 'You were my age when Dad died. When are you going to get it into your head that I'm an adult, w—'

'Not for another three weeks, you're not.'

'And another thing,' she steamrolled ahead. 'I've been...'

What the...? He blinked, refocused, Melissa's protests fading into the background somewhere. *His name was Jared, and this dream hottie could scorch her sheets any time he wanted—*

'Something wrong?'

'What?' He tore his eyes away momentarily to glimpse

Melissa staring at him. He shook his head, whether in denial or to clear it, he didn't know. 'It's nothing.' Nothing he wanted to share, least of all with his baby sister who'd just accused him of being conservative. *My snakeskin-print G-string melted away beneath the heat of his hand and my thighs fell apart as he—* Whoa.

He threw back a mouthful of the bubbly but the liquid did little to soothe his suddenly very dry, very tight throat. He set the glass down with a clunk.

'Bad news?'

'Not exactly…' Though what *exactly* this was, he didn't know. Yet. But he intended finding out.

'So, as I was saying, I've been giving it some thought, and—'

'Sorry, Liss, I'm going to have to deal with this,' he said, rising. He caught the frustration in her eyes but he couldn't give her his full attention until he'd resolved the hot little matter currently burning a hole in his palm. 'We'll talk later, okay?'

He headed straight for his study and booted up his computer. Drummed his fingers on the desk. The attachment was titled with today's date. No reference to Lygon.

He swiped his palms over day-old stubble, clicked the file open. The text flashed onto the screen. It was pink. Wild, colourful and erotic. Despite himself, he felt a smile tug the corner of his mouth. The more he read, the hotter it became.

The hotter *he* became.

He shifted on his chair to ease a growing pressure beneath the front of his trousers. The scene was so vivid he could almost feel the silky smoothness of her inner thighs, the budded nipple against his palm, her sultry heat as he plunged inside her.

When he'd finished, most of his blood had pooled in his lap. He leaned back, rolled tensed shoulders and shook his head to clear the images. He'd had no idea words alone could turn a man rock hard in less than a minute.

Man, he really needed to get laid.

Sophie Buchanan. Had he met her? He didn't recognise the name, but then he didn't always remember the names of women he'd slept with a few months after the fact. And it *had* been that long. His business and family made sure of that.

Snakeskin print. He grinned to himself. He'd definitely remember snakeskin. And he was pretty sure he'd have remembered that kinky position… Was it even anatomically possible? He was damn well willing to give it his best shot—given the opportunity…

So…Sophie Buchanan must have attached the wrong document to her email. Didn't stop him sending it to his printer. Should he ignore it tomorrow? Mention it to her? Tempting to watch her reaction, but, professionally speaking, in his place of business? Probably not.

She'd sent it thirty minutes ago, he noted. Had she been in bed? In her snakeskin G-string, perhaps. Lust hazed his vision, sweat slicked his palms, his brow, the back of his neck.

Steady, he ordered himself. Then another thought occurred to him. Was this some kind of set-up? Perhaps it was her intention to get him hot and bothered. What if she'd deliberately set out to seduce him? Looking for a more permanent position in his company via his bed. Disgust left a nasty taste in his mouth. Equally distasteful was the thought that she was attracted to his wealth and prepared to do anything to savour some of it.

The printer shot out the first page. That was when he noticed the minuscule print in the footer: *dreamdiary.*

A dream. Scanning the page, he nodded slowly and his smile returned. Okay, that made sense. Some woman's dream fantasy…and he'd been the star attraction. His smile widened to an all-out grin.

What did this woman look like? Masses of unruly wheat-blonde hair. A wickedly clever mouth. Overinflated breasts with large pink nipples. Sexy, supple and spontaneous. Sophie.

Still grinning, he folded the two steaming pages, tucked them in his pocket.

He was looking forward to tomorrow morning.

* * *

From her car parked nearby, Sophie stared through the windscreen of her Mazda hatch. The tall building's glass façade seemed to glint with power and authority in the early morning sunshine. The offices of J Sanderson Property Investments and Refurbishments occupied the top two floors.

Just the thought of what she had to do had her heart pounding into her throat, her fingers white-knuckled on the steering wheel. *He won't be there. Please don't let him be there.* She'd set his agenda yesterday and knew he had a breakfast meeting in Coolangatta, a thirty-minute drive away. He wasn't due at the office until 10:00 a.m.

Which didn't mean squat. In Sophie's experience bosses never did the expected.

She drew in a deep fortifying breath. *Get this over with.* Gripping her bag, she climbed out into the already balmy, salt-scented air, smoothed her fade-into-the-background beige knee-length skirt and headed for the building.

A few people were out on their morning jog along the wide stretch of beach, a soft aqua sea foamed along its edge. Not a suit or briefcase in sight. She checked her watch. Two minutes to seven. She'd not slept a wink, worrying about Jared Sanderson's reaction if he saw her email before she could delete it. If he hadn't already checked his emails from home, that was.

Don't even think about it.

Pam had complained the man never knew when to stop. Sophie's stomach dipped suddenly as if weighted down with a bag of that wet sand beyond, and she quickened her steps.

At the entrance, she fiddled with the collar of her white blouse, ensuring all but the top button was secure. She'd scrunched her thick long hair into a clasp at the back of her head.

She smiled a good morning to the security guy unlocking the door as she withdrew her swipe card from the pocket in the side of her bag and kept moving—not too fast so as to draw attention to herself—to the elevators.

A moment later she stepped out into the hushed Sanderson offices. Quickly skirting the main reception area, she crossed the oblique sun-striped carpet to Pam's desk, then slipped her handbag into the desk drawer.

The room was empty, still and so quiet she could hear the ocean's eternal shoosh beyond the thick glass windows. And the guilty echo of her pulse.

The swipe card gave her access to the Inner Sanctum but she'd not had a reason to enter yesterday. Today, however... Pushing the door open, she registered nothing beyond the scent of leather and electronics as she swooped on the only thing that mattered right now. His desk was L-shaped and the computer was positioned against the wall, which meant if he turned up she'd see him to her left.

She switched the machine on. Waited on a knife's edge. Because her legs were shaky, she barely hesitated before she sat down on his wide leather chair and rolled it forward. The faint fragrance of sandalwood met her nostrils, a heart-stopping reminder that this was a gross invasion of his privacy. She tapped in the password Pam had given her. The email icon appeared, she clicked on it, waiting, barely breathing while the messages rolled down the screen. *There*. Her email. Flagged as unread.

A noise, part sob, part laugh, mostly relief, escaped her as with two swift clicks she deleted the email permanently. Done. Simple.

She leaned back, blew out a long slow breath while her heart continued to thump like crazy against her ribs. I.T. security never audited executive email. Did they?

She would *not* think about that now. She hit the keyboard and brought his day's agenda up on screen. All she had to do was slip back to her desk and no one would—

'Good morning.' The deep masculine voice steamrolled over her senses like steel wrapped in black velvet.

She couldn't have leapt out of the chair quicker if she'd been shot at. Her mind scrambled for words—any words—but to her mortification all that came out was the sound of air rushing past her tonsils.

She got an impression of height, power and stunning sexuality while a pair of enigmatic olive-green eyes studied her. And her stomach dropped to her professional, low-heeled, slingback shoes.

'Ms Buchanan, I presume?'

CHAPTER TWO

How long had he been standing there?

'Yes… Ah… Sophie…' she managed, two stuttering heartbeats later. 'Sophie Buchanan.'

And, oh…he was *gorgeous*, from the sun-bleached tips of his dark brown hair to that clean-shaven jaw that looked strong enough to crack rocks on. From the pressed white shirt and charcoal tie to the fresh sandalwood soap scent winding through her senses. She didn't dare let her gaze wander down the rest of him.

He was the kind of man that made you momentarily forget your own name because you were too busy drawing breath and taking in the view.

For heaven's sake, you could be in serious trouble here, girl. Focus. She dragged the scattered remnants of her business self together. 'Good morning…Mr Sanderson…I was just…I've brought your agenda…up.' Then, as if she hadn't just been hacking into his computer without his knowledge, she walked smartly around from behind his desk, stuck out her hand. Smiled. And, for once, thanked the genes that had bestowed her with a five-feet-ten height advantage—but still it wasn't enough because this man was at least six feet two. 'I'm looking forward to working with you today.'

His firm unyielding palm met hers—an instant zap—and she had to force herself not to think about the way he'd palmed her breasts in her dream last night.

Because nothing surer, this *was* that guy.

And that was bad. Very bad. She didn't *want* her dream lover spilling into her working life and she needed every day's employment she could get. How was she going to face him all day today and not remember how it felt to be made mad, passionate and sizzling love to? And more importantly, not to let it show?

At least he didn't know. He couldn't... Or did he? One corner of his mouth stretched into some semblance of a smile but the eyes...there was a lot going on behind those shadowed green eyes...

'Call me Jared,' he said, still imprisoning her hand within his large firm grip. 'We keep things informal around here.'

Yes, very informal. Smile still frozen in place, she tugged her fingers from his grasp, clasped her tingling hand at her side and reminded herself that he hadn't bothered to introduce himself yesterday. 'Right. Jared—' She practically bit off the word and pressed her lips together. She had *not* just moaned his name the way she had last night, but guilty heat streaked into her cheeks anyway. He was only speaking to her now because she was in his office.

To delete an email from his computer.

The screen of which he was studying, brows lowered. Against her will, her eyes flicked there too, to make sure the file hadn't somehow popped up again. When she looked back at him he was studying her with that same inscrutable expression.

He seemed to shake it away and said, 'I apologise for missing you yesterday, I had to rush off. My sister went into labour and her husband was unavoidably detained. I trust Mimi looked after you?'

The receptionist. 'Yes, she did.' Sophie instantly forgave him for yesterday's lapse. How many guys were so involved with their sisters that they'd rush off to be with them during labour? Unlike her brother, who'd not contacted her since he'd escaped the hell that was their home and moved to Melbourne years ago.

'Did everything go okay?' she said, relieved to have something other than that dreaded email and the sexual buzz that seemed to surround them to focus on. 'What did she have?'

His eyes warmed and, oh, my, he had the most disarmingly crooked grin that kind of creased his left cheek and threatened to buckle her knees.

'Everything went great.' If he'd been the father he couldn't have sounded more delighted. 'It's a girl. Arabella. Three and a half kilos or seven pounds seven ounces in the old money.'

'Wonderful. Lovely name.' She paused. 'So I guess you were busy last night, then. Celebrating?' *Far too busy to catch up on boring old matters such as emails from the office.*

He looked at her with an unsettling directness, as if he'd heard her thoughts. Indeed, as if he knew what she'd been enjoying last night, with him. And more of that blood pumped into her cheeks.

He smiled again, that warmth back in his eyes. 'Melissa and I had a champagne or two.'

Melissa? He was involved. Sophie felt as if something had jabbed her skin and left her deflating piece by piece. She had to force her shoulders back and stand straight. Pam hadn't let her in on that little snippet. She'd told her he didn't have time for relationships, his family took precedence, that women were way down on his list, and, no, he wasn't gay.

Sophie reminded herself quickly and sternly that it made no difference. In fact it was good. Great. Men were off her agenda for life. And she was going overseas in three weeks and five days.

She lifted her chin to demonstrate a confidence she was far from feeling. 'I won't hold you up. I know you have an eight a.m. meeting in Coolangatta.' Thank heavens. She could—

'No rush,' he said in that steel and velvet voice that both startled and enticed.

'I...' She watched the way the muscles in his back shifted beneath the smooth white cotton as he sank into his plush leather chair. Held her breath and waited for her heart to stop while she watched his long tanned fingers work the keyboard and… *Oh, dear*… Remembered those clever fingers working on her body… The sensation peppered her skin with instant goose-bumps.

She shook the fantasy away. More important to worry about how long he'd been watching her at his desk and what he'd seen. From her position, she saw him click off his agenda and bring up his emails. Her stomach tightened. Oh, *no*.

'Wouldn't want to miss anything important…' He glanced sideways at her, although how a glance could scour your eyes for every secret you'd ever kept and last for eternity—

Prickly heat climbed up her neck and her hand rose unsteadily to play with the button at her throat. 'I'll let you get on with it,' she said, backing away before he decided to open his Deleted Items folder and flash her private thoughts onto the screen and…she'd just die of embarrassment. No, no, she reminded her stunned self, she'd deleted it permanently. She was off the hook—

'What's this?' He stilled, leaning closer to the screen, blocking Sophie's view and her heart jumped into her mouth again. 'This is your work, I take it?' He turned slowly towards her. His eyes seemed darker and there was a gleam there that she was sure hadn't been there before.

She found herself backing away from his powerful gaze as if pushed by some physical force. Her hands alternately fluttered and clenched in front of her. 'I can…explain…'

'No need.' He leaned back in his chair, a slow smile touching his lips. 'I left it with Pam but I see you've finished it. Everything looks to be in order, you can email it today.'

The Lygon report. A sigh escaped her lips, instantly bitten off when she caught him still watching her, eyes darker than she'd thought. She straightened. 'I'll get right on it.'

'This afternoon will be soon enough.' He glanced back at the screen, then said, 'Nothing else here that can't wait.'

He rose and she almost sagged with relief. Her legs were like jelly and she really, really wanted to escape to her desk and regroup.

But before she could propel herself forward—rather, backward and away—he opened his briefcase, pulled out a few files. 'Since you're here and obviously enthusiastic to get on with the day, I'd like you to come with me.'

'Me?' *To Coolangatta? With him?* Her breath caught. 'But…'

He looked up sharply. 'Is that a problem?'

Uh oh. A temporary PA's golden rule: do not irritate the boss no matter how short your stay is. 'No. Not at all. Absolutely.' She shook her head, then nodded. Her head spun.

'Good.' His eyes pinned hers so directly, so intensely, she felt as if she were being probed, naked, with twin lasers.

She flicked at her collar, lifted her blouse away from her skin, sticky now despite her morning shower, and flashed him a smile. 'I'll leave a note for Mimi.'

'Fine.' He blinked, then seemed to shake his head, the movement abrupt, and frowned at his watch. 'Better make that call from the car on the way.' He handed Sophie the files without looking at her. 'These need mailing this afternoon.' His voice was clipped as he snapped his case shut. 'Bring Pam's laptop, you can familiarise yourself with the project before we get there. Coffee— Forget it, we don't have time.'

'No worries.' *This* was more like the Jared Sanderson Pam had talked about. Complained about. Adjusting the files in her arms, she swung around to carry them to her desk. 'I'll meet you downstairs in two minutes…'

But he was already out of the door, leaving that spicy fragrance in his wake.

Jared tossed his briefcase and suit jacket onto the back seat of his new pride and joy, his BMW hard-topped convertible, and blew out a strained breath. Took off his cufflinks, slid them into his trouser pocket and rolled his sleeves up—something he never did before meeting a new client. He was a professional and he dressed like one. Every day. He liked routine, the predictability of it.

There was nothing routine about this morning.

Nor was Sophie Buchanan, dream-weaver, what he'd expected. Unlike the brazen and over-endowed vision he'd imagined, she was tall, slim and understated. She wasn't his usual blonde; her hair was the colour of a mid-winter's night. Smooth and sleek and shiny.

He hadn't missed her fragrance on the air when she'd all but leapt off his chair. Not the expensive perfume most women he knew wore, but something light and sparkly, like fresh fruit and summer.

And all he'd been able to see when they'd made eye contact was the disturbing image of her sprawled over his bed wearing nothing but a blackberry-stained smile and dangling a sliver of snakeskin from one finger. It had taken considerable restraint not to yank her against him and find out if the reality was as good as the fantasy she'd described.

She'd deleted the email.

He'd seen the nerves, read the body language and was confident it had been a genuine mistake, not some scheme she'd devised to get his attention.

The devil of it was it *had* got his attention, and in a big way. Just looking at her and knowing what she'd been dreaming had given him a hard-on and he was still feeling its effects. Not a professional image. And knowing all those intimate details, how was he going to deal with having her right outside his office all day?

So why had he asked her to accompany him to Coolangatta? He couldn't resist the smile. Maybe because she was here already and his PA usually accompanied him? The smile teased his lips into a full-on grin. Maybe he wasn't going to change his routine just because Pam was unavailable?

And maybe he wanted to find out more about Sophie

Buchanan. Like why this woman had dreamed sexy dreams about him when they hadn't even met. The trick would be not mixing business and pleasure.

She exited the building, sunshine sparking off her ebony hair as she searched his car out. Unlike her fantasy, her dress code was wishy-washy conservative, but a gust of wind blew the fabric of her blouse against her body, outlining a low-cut bra and subtle yet teasing curves. He leaned across the seat and shoved open the passenger door, slid on his sunglasses and fiddled with his GPS while he waited—hardly courteous, but it was preferable to the alternative of letting her see how she'd affected him.

How her *creative writing* had affected him.

So he wouldn't let the way he'd noticed her hips undulate provocatively as she crossed the car park—not to mention those long tanned legs beneath her fitted skirt—distract his thoughts from the upcoming meeting.

She dropped into the passenger seat as if those spectacular legs were about to give out and he grinned to himself. Dying to know if he knew, wasn't she? But she wasn't asking, and he wasn't telling.

'Been temping long?' he asked as he swung out of the car park.

'A few years. But not for much longer.' He noted she wasted no time opening the laptop.

'Why's that?'

She tapped keys, her attention riveted to the screen. 'I'm going to the UK next month.'

'Oh? Working or sightseeing?'

'Both, I hope.'

'Anything lined up there?'

'Work-wise, not yet. I'll take it as it comes.'

They were cruising south along the Gold Coast Highway, negotiating the morning peak-hour traffic, and he wondered for a moment how it would feel to take off across the globe with no responsibilities and only oneself to think about.

'We'll be meeting with the building's owner and the architect to discuss the project brief,' he informed her. 'You'll find the info in the file labelled CoolCm20. Familiarise yourself with it and be prepared to add to it later.'

They followed the bitumen past Burleigh Heads and crossed the bridge where a glimpse of turquoise water met white sand lined with Norfolk pines. Salty air with a whiff of motor fumes blew through the open window, but at this time of day he preferred the fresh morning breeze to air conditioning.

'So your company offers clients advice on refurbishment projects,' she said, looking up from the file a short time later.

He nodded, checking his rear-view mirror before changing lanes. 'Not only advice. We prepare a complete project brief. Should he or she wish to proceed, we initiate contracts and manage the project to completion.' He glanced her way. 'So you and Pam know each other?'

She nodded. 'We go back a long way. As a matter of fact, we're still neighbours in the same apartment complex.'

'You're from Newcastle too, then.'

'Yes. I moved up here four years ago.'

'With family?'

She shook her head and looked away towards the side window.

'Boyfriend? Partner?' he asked, glancing her way again when she didn't elaborate. He saw her shoulders tense, her jaw tighten.

'I needed a change of scenery,' was all she said.

Obviously it wasn't only the scenery she'd wanted to change. Someone had hurt her. None of his business, Jared told himself. He didn't need to know her life history. He was only interested in the Sophie who was sitting beside him right now. The one who smelled as fresh as the morning and dreamed about him.

He couldn't help the smile that threatened to give him away every time he thought about it. The idea of this quietly professional woman playing out those erotic fantasies with him had grasped him firmly between his thighs and wasn't about to let go.

Unless he did something about it…

Change of scenery. If only it had been that simple. Sophie refocused her gaze on the safety of the computer screen. How could she have stayed in Newcastle knowing she might bump into Glen and his new lover—his new *pregnant* lover? Which was inevitable given their mutual friends and working environments. She hadn't wanted their pitying glances and platitudes so she'd moved to the Gold Coast and taken a business course.

But recurring childhood nightmares had continued to hound her, screwing with her life, making her ill until she'd had no alternative but to seek professional help. Her counsellor had suggested a dream diary and they'd used it to work through her emotional issues. Her abused childhood, her failure as a woman. Even the fact that she'd sought help was still, to her, a failure.

She'd come a long way since arriving in Surfers but the past still haunted her at the oddest times. A word tossed out and she was back in her childhood purgatory, her disastrous marriage. Nightmares were few and far between these days but she still recorded her dreams. A security thing, she supposed.

At least Jared had taken the hint and not pursued further conversation as the car sped south. It gave her a moment to shake off the bad. The bad was gone, over, done, she reminded herself. As Roma had told her at her final session, *good times ahead*. And that was what it was all about, right? Refocusing on the present, Sophie resumed her attention to the upcoming meeting.

She reread the document on the screen for the umpteenth time. She couldn't remember a darn word. It was as if her mind had shut out everything except her awareness of the man beside her. Right now his forearm relaxed on the steering wheel. Suntanned, sprinkled with dark hair and sporting an expensive-looking watch, ropes of sinew shifting as he swung out from behind a truck and changed lanes.

She jerked her eyes back to the screen. This infatuation, or whatever it was, was not going to get her paid at the end of the day. She reminded herself he was unavailable. Involved with someone else. Focused on family and his high-flying career. And most important: she wasn't interested in getting involved.

It should have been easy to push it aside and if it hadn't been for that stupid dream this whole attraction thing never would have happened. Would it?

'No special guy, then?'

The question asked in that deep voice jerked her out of her self-talk and put her immediately on the defensive. She focused her gaze on the road ahead. 'I don't see how having a man in my life is relevant to my ability to do my job.'

He was silent for a beat, as if considering her snarky response. Then he said, 'I generally find women in steady relationships make for more stable employees.'

'Only women?' How sexist was that? But she didn't say it. She'd done enough damage in the past twelve hours. She just wanted to do her job with a minimum of fuss and attention and get paid at the end of the day. Then she never had to see him again.

'Rest assured, I have a strong and committed work ethic, Mr Sanderson—Jared. And while we're on the topic, how about women in *no* relationship?'

And why the heck had she said that? Was her subconscious *trying* to get her into trouble?

With smooth efficiency, he overtook a shiny red Porsche. 'Which category do you fall into?'

'Does it matter?'

'It might.'

A sharp excitement stabbed through her, followed closely by one of anger. She forgot her decision not to look at him. His profile—his very strong, very masculine profile—betrayed no clue as to what he was thinking. 'What do you mean "it might"?'

What about Melissa? Did he think she'd forgotten? Not noticed? No matter how gorgeous his looks, no matter what she'd fantasised, she did *not* play the other woman. She knew how it felt to be left for someone else.

'I need to know whether you're expected home this evening,' he continued as they neared their destination. 'I missed work yesterday, which means we'll need to work late tonight to catch up.'

'Oh.' The barely audible word escaped her lips as the implication sank in. Just him and her alone in his office. To catch up on *work*. How ridiculously foolish and pathetic she was, to have assumed he'd had something more on his mind.

'No one's expecting me. I live alone.' She hoped her face wasn't as pink as it felt. Still, it wouldn't have mattered since he didn't even glance her way.

'You don't have other plans, I hope.'

'No.' And from his tone she rather gathered that she'd have had to cancel if she had. Pam had warned her the man was work-driven and focused and expected the same of his staff.

'Which reminds me…' He indicated his phone on the console between them while he adjusted his earpiece. 'Get Melissa for me, please. She's on speed dial.'

'Melissa.' Her stomach dipped, clenched, but she did as he requested, then turned away and watched the scenery slip by. High-rise apartments and businesses interspersed with strips of green and pandanus trees and now glimpses of blue sea. She wouldn't allow herself to feel uncomfortable.

'Lissa, hi, it's me. I won't be home for tea, I'm working back.' Brisk and to the point. Pause. 'I don't have time to talk about that now, Liss. I have someone with me.' He lifted his sunglasses to rub the bridge of his nose. 'Later. And tell Cryssie I'll call by the hospital tomorrow for sure. Yeah. Bye.'

Sophie couldn't pretend she hadn't heard the conversation. The way that smooth tone had roughened with something that sounded close to exasperation.

'My sister,' he muttered.

A tiny shiver danced down her spine and she remained motionless a moment, lips pressed together to stop the smile threatening at the corners of her mouth and trying not to feel ridiculously…what? Pleased? Excited? Delighted?

She shouldn't be feeling any of those things.

Leather creaked as he shifted in his seat. She saw the movement from the corner of her eye, saw him glance at her as he exhaled an impatient breath through his nostrils. 'I fail to see the humour. Ever tried reasoning with a seventeen-year-old girl?'

Her smile bubbled over into a laugh and she glanced his way. Clenched jaw. Hands a little tight on the steering wheel. Speedo a little high as they cruised along the esplanade and into Coolangatta. 'Can't say I have. But I've been one, so I can tell you it does get better.'

He made some non-committal noise as he pulled to a stop outside a four-storey apartment block and switched off the ignition. 'It can be a challenge at times.'

He spoke as if he were Melissa's parent rather than her brother. Or maybe it was just that brothers were never meant to get along with their sisters. Yet she knew that wasn't true. The dysfunctional household she'd been brought up in had tainted and distorted her perception of family life and love.

'Do you have siblings?' His voice interrupted her thoughts.

'A brother. In Melbourne.'

Somewhat surprised by her instant switch from bright and chirpy to gloom and doom, Jared reached for his jacket on the back seat. 'You're not close?'

She followed his lead, gathering her bag and laptop. 'I haven't seen him in years, so no.' She peered through the windscreen at the nondescript grey building behind a cyclone fence. 'This is the place?'

'Yep.'

Jared had been itching to get another good look at her since they'd left Surfers but the traffic had been snarly and required his full attention. Now he took a moment. The brandy-coloured eyes had lost that desperation he'd seen in his office and he doubted the hint of blush on her high wide cheekbones was make-up—more likely her natural colour. And her lips... they were something else. Full, luscious-looking and caramel glossed...they promised to taste as sweet...

Damn it, not now.

He reminded himself this wasn't a date, ordered his unruly body to cooperate and forced his attention to the building in front of them while he rolled down his sleeves. 'You have to think potential, Sophie.'

He'd made his fortune by seeing possibilities and making them happen. He'd been a millionaire at twenty-seven because he dared to dream and didn't let others tell him it wasn't possible.

'I'm afraid I'm not very imaginative.'

His gaze swung back to her just as she turned to him with a stunned tell-me-I-didn't-say-that expression and their gazes locked and for a beat out of time the spectre of that dream fantasy smouldered in the tiny space between them. 'I don't believe that for a moment.'

'Believe it,' she muttered, and, pushing out of the car, she started walking.

He shrugged into his jacket, grabbed his briefcase from the back seat and caught up with her along the path. Without further comment she accompanied him to the main door where they met the owner, Sam Trent, and Ben Harbison, an architect who'd worked with Jared on several projects. After a briefing in Sam's office, they spent half an hour inspecting the premises while Sophie took notes. For the remainder of the meeting, she worked unobtrusively at one end of the table, the only sound the quiet click of her keyboard.

Unobtrusive? For the second time in as many minutes Jared looked up from the plans in front of him, his gaze unerringly finding Sophie. Focused on her task, she wasn't giving him a second's glance.

How did she manage cool concentration when he couldn't? Her fast, efficient fingers with their clear-varnished nails were the cause of the clicking and Jared couldn't stop thinking about them being fast and efficient in other ways, as she'd described in her dream. And whenever the breeze wafted through the open window, it wasn't the sea air but her fragrance that floated to his nostrils.

The meeting wrapped up at nine-fifteen. He was glad his ten o'clock appointment didn't require his PA. And his eleven-fifteen would keep him busy until lunch. Only the afternoon to get through, he thought, watching the little hollows behind her knees as she bent over to retrieve her bag from the floor.

Swinging his gaze away, he focused on Sam's conversation while he stuffed a couple of files into his briefcase. Reminded himself again that he didn't get involved with employees.

However, a couple of hours of working back this evening would clear yesterday's clutter and when the work was finished Sophie's two-day fill-in for Pam would be over. She would no longer be in his employ…

CHAPTER THREE

'YOUR ten o'clock cancelled,' Sophie informed Jared as they walked to the car.

A hunger fist clenched around her stomach. She hadn't had time for breakfast. And she'd refused Sam's offer for refreshment because she hadn't been sure she'd keep it down she was so uptight, and had stuck to her bottled water. 'He'll ring back this afternoon and reschedule.'

Jared aimed the remote at the car and the alarm blipped. 'In that case, I'd like to make another stop before we head back.'

She'd been hoping for some time and space back at the office. Alone at her desk. She didn't want to be anywhere near him, inhaling his scent, listening to his voice and wondering… This on-the-edge-of-the-seat feeling that Jared might have read her diary was killing her. In a way it was almost worse than knowing. At least if she knew, she could make some attempt to deal with it. But she wasn't going to risk asking.

It was a beautiful day with the sky's blue dome reflecting on the sea. Ridges of surf scrolled along the sand, already dotted with beach-goers. Right now Sophie wished she were one of them. No boss to stress over, just a day of relaxation stretched out to enjoy. Or better still, to be one of the gulls wheeling high and low over the ocean.

As she watched Jared open the boot she reminded herself she'd be as free as those gulls in just under four weeks. He dropped his gear in, motioned her to do the same with Pam's laptop. He shrugged out of his jacket once more, then to her surprise he yanked off his tie and tossed it in the boot with the rest of his stuff, and said, 'What do you say to fish and chips?'

Now? What was wrong with muesli and fruit and a nice hot coffee? 'It's only nine-twenty—'

'First off, do you like fish and chips? And I'm not talking the fast-food skinny-mini deals but the old-fashioned crisp on the outside, soft in the middle and wrapped in butcher paper kind.'

'I do, but—'

'So forget the office—and the boss—for an hour and take a break. I know a little seafood shop here that's open early. They do take-away cappuccino too, if you need your caffeine fix.'

Forget the office? Take a break? She'd barely done an hour's work. Forgetting the boss wasn't going to happen and fish and chips at nine-thirty on a weekday?

Was this happy-looking, suddenly smiling man the same man Pam said was all work and no play? There had to be a catch.

'O-k-ay.' She smiled back, blinded by that knee-weakening crease. It really should be registered as a deadly weapon.

One block back from the esplanade and a few moments' walk brought them to a row of shops. They passed a bakery and its rich scent of coffee and fresh bread. Sophie slowed her steps, all but drooling at the window selection, but then Jared laid a casual hand on her shoulder.

She jumped at the startling contact as he steered her past the shop with barely there persuasion. It seemed an easy relaxed gesture, except that she was super aware of the slight pressure of his fingers on her collarbone, like a low-grade current tickling her flesh. Aware also of the sun-warmed fragrances of clean cotton and masculine skin surrounding her.

As if he knew she'd been about to forgo chips in ten minutes in favour of a sticky bun *right now*, he dipped his head and said, 'It'll be worth the wait.' His voice was lazy and layered with all the richness of the Black Forest gateau she'd just salivated over.

'Is that a promise?' She heard her own voice echo that same tone and her suddenly dry tongue cleaved to the roof of her mouth. Her heart rate accelerated as she turned and looked up at him. They *were* talking food, weren't they?

His expression revealed nothing...but had his eyes gone darker? 'You can tell me afterwards.'

'Right.' His eyes *were* darker. And up close she noticed the distinctive olive green was ringed with a fine rim of navy. She also noticed they'd stopped walking. He was still touching her and her flesh was still tingling.

She hitched her bag higher so that his hand slid away, and resumed walking, but he was close enough so that their arms bumped, a too-delicious friction of firm flesh, crisp shirt and masculine hair.

A moment later he slowed again, this time outside a bright shop called The Baby Tree with teddies spilling out of prams and the cutest little baby outfits suspended from colourful chains. 'Come on. Help me choose something for my new niece. Thirty seconds. What do you think—a teddy or that fluffy red kangaroo?'

For one trembly moment of indecision Sophie stared at the pretty window and the pair of tiny overalls covered in roses with a matching sunhat. The rainbow selection of lace booties. And yearned.

Then the familiar chill that accompanied such visions swirled through her heart and she shivered in the balmy air. She hadn't set foot in a baby shop since— In a long time.

'I'm not really a baby person.' She spun away from the window and gazed at the shop across the street, but didn't see it. 'Don't let me stop you, though.' Without looking at him, she dredged up a smile from somewhere and pasted it on her lips, while groping in her bag for her sunglasses. Hoping she looked more careless and indifferent than she felt, she waved in the direction they'd been heading. 'I'll go ahead and order.'

She slid on the glasses, turned and walked. *One foot in front of the other.* Her smile dropped from her lips and she was conscious of the residual sweaty palms and heavy heartbeat. Of all the shops he could have chosen, he'd stopped at The Baby Tree.

It had caught her off guard. With most of her friends down the coast in Newcastle, over the past four years it had been easy to avoid the baby trap. Pam was seriously single and Sophie's focus was her upcoming overseas trip. *Not* making babies and playing happy families.

Those things hadn't worked for her.

She'd be ready next time he pulled that trick. Next time? She coughed out a half-laugh. Hardly. After today she wouldn't have to see Jared Sanderson again. She kept her eyes peeled for the fish shop, but she hadn't gone farther than a couple of metres along the footpath when he caught up.

He fell into step beside her. 'Hey.'

His tone was bland and she couldn't decide if he was annoyed or concerned. Please, God, anything but concern. She could deal with annoyance, indifference, even anger, but concern… Concern could weaken her resistance, leaving her vulnerable. Again. She refused to allow anyone too close. Giving your love, your trust, yourself to someone else only brought heartbreak. She'd learned that lesson too.

Jared must have caught the vibes; he'd put at least an arm span between them and guilt pierced the self-preservation she normally surrounded herself with. 'I really don't mind. She's your sister… If you want to—'

'No big deal, I'll do it later. We're here.' He stopped at the next wide glass door and pushed it open, the air-conditioned swirl mingling with the aroma of hot fat.

'Rico. *Buongiorno.*'

'*Buongiorno.*' The rotund swarthy man beaming at Jared as

if he was some long-lost friend looked to be in his late forties. He also looked as if he'd been dining on his own menu for a good many of those years. 'Didn't expect to see you down this way today.'

'Had a spare hour.'

'And you haven't come alone.' He shone his beam on Sophie.

'Rico, meet Sophie. Sophie, Rico. A serve of your best chips to go, please, my friend. And a cappuccino for my hard-working colleague here.'

'Very happy to make your acquaintance, Sophie.' Rico winked at her as he scooped chips into a wire basket, lowered it into the fryer. 'If this man doesn't treat you right, I have a brother. Has his own seafood restaurant in Broadbeach. He's single and better looking.'

Sophie shoved her sunglasses on top of her head. She glanced at Jared, caught him looking at her and didn't quite smother her grin. 'I'll keep it in mind.'

'Get Jared to take you there for dinner one night.'

She jerked her gaze back to Rico. 'Oh…no. I'm…we're not… dating.'

His thick black brows rose, then a look of pure devilment danced in his dark eyes. 'Why not?'

'I'm just temping at Jared's office for the day…' Why had she said the D word, for heaven's sake? Rico had no doubt meant a business dinner. But it had just burst out…and, oh, she wished the floor would open up and swallow her.

'Don't listen to him, Sophie,' Jared said, his voice tinged with amusement, and to Rico, 'Did you go over those figures with Enzo yet?'

And just what had Jared meant by that look he'd given Rico? To her relief, he seemed to have forgotten she was there already. To keep from feeling like a spare part and to give them some privacy since they were discussing business, she crossed to one of the little round tables by the window, sat down and flicked through a well-thumbed women's magazine.

Anything to keep from looking at him. Or admiring the cut to the trousers that showcased long legs and firm butt and imagining… *No.* Frowning, she forced herself to refocus on the latest celebrity break-up.

Her eyes remained on the page but her mind worked as the guys talked. The familiarity and bond between the two was obvious. Jared hadn't taken an hour out of his day to 'forget about the office' and entertain her. He'd used the opportunity to catch up with Rico and make it seem as if he were doing Sophie a favour at the same time. Very clever.

'Bring your coffee,' he said, dragging her out of her contemplation, 'and let's go see the beach.'

They took their white paper-wrapped package to the esplanade and sat on a bench overlooking the sand. The sea's *boom-dump* vibrated through the soles of her feet. The gulls swooped in noisily from nowhere the moment Sophie unwrapped the shared snack. She took a chip, broke it open, popped a piece in her mouth. Then she threw the other half to the birds to watch them squawk and squabble while she sipped at her much anticipated frothy cappuccino.

'You're right, they're yummy,' she said, reaching for another while carefully avoiding Jared's fingers. She hadn't eaten chips this good since she couldn't remember when.

'Haven't done this in a while,' Jared said, popping the top on his can of soda.

'Probably just as well. Salt, fat, calories. Too much of a good thing…'

Sophie watched, mesmerised as he downed his cola in deep slow swallows that made his Adam's apple bob amazingly. He lifted his lips from the can a moment and smiled, eyes twinkling. 'You can never have too much of a good thing, Sophie.'

Oh, the way he said that, all luscious and low as if he was talking about sex. And drawing her attention to his lips, wet with the cola…and they'd be cool and sweet…

Not going there.

She plucked another fat, fragrant chip, slid it between her lips and, closing her eyes, savoured every drop of excess. If she couldn't have sex, at least she could eat. 'So…' Licking the salt from her fingers, she opened her eyes once more to find him still watching her. More precisely, watching her mouth. 'That's your opinion and you're sticking to it.'

'A good thing is only a good thing for as long as you enjoy it.'

Glen had lived by that code too, Sophie remembered. She drained her coffee to mask the sudden bitterness in her mouth. 'Then what? You discard it for another passing fancy?'

'If it's not bringing you pleasure, then yeah.'

Her fingers tightened around the polystyrene cup. 'Sounds totally self-absorbed to me.'

He laughed. 'Probably. And why not? So long as it's not hurting anyone else…'

'Exactly.' She relented. Okay, maybe he didn't include relationships in that particular philosophy. It seemed he genuinely cared about people. Rico. His sisters. Even Pam. He was one of the good guys after all. And mega rich, mega gorgeous, mega motivated.

She noticed his gaze had turned speculative and probing. Something glimmered in the green depths and her heart skipped a beat. Did he read minds as well? Looking away, she took aim and tossed her empty cup neatly into the trash can.

'What about your favourites list? What can't you have too much of, Sophie?'

You. Naked. Inside me.

Her skin warmed, prickled, and she swore every internal organ turned to mush. She felt like an over-ripe peach, ready to be plucked, split apart and plundered. Gloriously and within an inch of her life.

Liquid heat gathered between her thighs and she bit the inside of her lip. Had she just accused *him* of being self-absorbed? Behind her sunglasses she met his unshielded gaze and reminded herself of what she really wanted these days. 'Wealth,' she said, reaching for the bottled water in her bag. She sucked it down with a vengeance. 'And independence.'

He looked surprised, as if he'd expected her to say something indulgent or female, like chocolate or shoes. A crease dug a groove between his brows. 'Sounds a little sad and lonely.'

'Why?' Annoyed with his response, she tipped her bottle in his direction. 'You don't strike me as lonely. Or sad. You've obviously worked towards those same goals all your life, and by all accounts you've succeeded better than most.' Which made him a hypocrite or sexist or both. 'So don't tell me you're not happy with your success.'

'That goes without saying and I assume you're talking financial success. But mostly I'm happy because I don't allow myself to think any other way. Doesn't mean I don't have my disappointments.'

Not knowing how to respond, she nodded as she reached for another chip. With his wealth and charisma, she'd not thought of Jared as a man to experience setbacks. Which was totally naïve of her. Everyone had setbacks. It was how one dealt with them.

He gave the impression that he was powerful enough to accomplish whatever he wanted, but she knew nothing of his background or what obstacles he'd overcome to get to where he was.

Before she could form a question around that, he said, 'I take it family and kids figure somewhere in all that wealth and independence.'

A few years ago Sophie's answer would have been an unequivocal yes. Despite the emotional trauma she'd experienced growing up in a family where booze and violence were the norm, she'd always believed it could be different for her. All those years of growing up with her collection of dolls and romantic ever afters, but now...

Reality check.

For the second time in less than an hour a reminder that her female body had let her down in the baby-making department. Which was hardly relevant since she had no intention of getting serious with a man, ever again. Still, it was failure and she chugged on her water bottle to take a moment to compose herself.

She pushed herself up from the bench, grateful for her sunglasses shield. 'Not me.' She laughed, turning seaward and throwing her hands wide. 'Why tie yourself down with kids when you can travel the world? Do what you choose when you choose. Live life the way you want.' She turned to him and nodded. 'Yes, I'm completely and unashamedly selfish. I admit it.'

Shading his forehead with a hand, Jared studied her through eyes squinted against the beach's glare. Hard to tell if she was being completely truthful because he couldn't read her eyes behind her sunglasses. Thanks to her, he'd left his own damn sunglasses in the car. She'd thrown him off course last night with her dream, and twelve hours later nothing had changed.

'Good for you,' he said, crushing the empty chip wrapper and standing too. 'I like an honest woman who's not afraid to say what she means.'

Why not take her at her word? he decided. He had no reason not to. So she admitted she was selfish—didn't matter to him in the great scheme of things. Besides, he had a feeling she wasn't as self-absorbed as she let on. He picked up his empty cola can and headed for the bin. 'It's time to make a move.'

At least she was upfront about what she wanted, he mused as they drove back to Surfers. Rico was right—Sophie was a beautiful woman. And red hot to boot. He'd not had a woman in too long, which was why his skin felt as if it were on fire and he couldn't for the life of him, get her out of his head. Beautiful. Single. Living in the moment.

Bianca had been the same, he remembered, with her wild sensual beauty and Bohemian lifestyle. God only knew why— when he thought about it with the wisdom of five years more maturity—but he'd fancied himself in love and had asked her to marry him.

But Bianca had refused to accept twelve-year-old Melissa as part of the deal. Something Jared didn't compromise on was Melissa's well-being, so it had been bye-bye Bianca.

After he'd picked up the pieces of his heart and fitted them back together, he'd realised he and Bianca would never have made it work in the long term.

But circumstances were different now. Melissa was more or less independent even if she did still live at home. So...if he and Sophie got together... From the outset he knew Sophie wasn't going to be long term. She was going overseas, so there was no possibility of anything serious developing between them.

Not that he could ever get serious with a happy wanderer who didn't like kids. He wasn't looking for marriage right now, but when he settled down he wanted a woman who held the same values he did. A lifetime commitment to family. Sharing, trust. And children.

But that wasn't now.

A few weeks with no-strings Sophie wouldn't be a hardship. Wouldn't be a hardship at all... He just had to seduce Sophie a little, tempt her with a taste of her own desires, her private fantasies... He ran a hand around the back of his neck, shifted on the seat as his blood pumped a little faster around his body. Then a smile touched his lips. Who knew her desires better than him? Who better than Jared to make those fantasies a reality?

CHAPTER FOUR

MEETINGS took up the rest of the morning. In the afternoon Jared escorted a millionaire businessman from Dubai and his entourage on a tour of inspection of a dozen complexes and resorts. Negotiations followed over a late lunch in one of Surfers Paradise's top restaurants.

He'd left Sophie an overflowing outbox and several reports to edit, file, print, mail.

Jared would be the first to acknowledge that Pam was a brilliant PA. She knew her stuff, was ruthlessly efficient, indispensable, in fact, and he'd hate to lose her. But he had to admit that behind her desk she tended to merge into the background.

Not Sophie Buchanan.

On his return at five-thirty, before he reached his office he could smell that sparkling fresh fragrance that had been spinning inside his head all day, making him think inappropriate thoughts. Taking his focus away from work.

Instead of concentrating on ways to convince Najeeb Assad that transforming an aging condominium building into a slice of paradise was a sound business decision, Jared had been visualising Sophie astride him on his office chair, her fragrant skin glowing with a sheen of sweat while she rode him hard and fast…

To Jared's relief, Mr Assad had concurred with his suggestions for renovation, but it could easily have gone the other way—and that concerned him. Jared had never allowed himself or his work to be sidetracked by a woman before.

It reinforced his belief that it was an idiot boss who got personally involved with his employees. So he afforded Sophie only a brief acknowledgement on his way through late in the afternoon, issuing a practical, 'Can I see you in my office with those reports you worked on yesterday in thirty minutes, please?'

Blowing out a breath, he dropped into his chair. With Pam due back tomorrow, he needed to go over yesterday's work with Sophie. But in a couple of hours he could loosen up and enjoy getting to know her better. On a more personal level.

Meanwhile he pulled out this afternoon's paperwork, skimmed it before setting it aside and working through the day's emails. From his position he couldn't see her beyond his door, but he could hear her moving around, the sounds of her desk drawer opening, closing.

Five minutes before she was due, the quick *rat-a-tat* had him half rising as he looked up from his screen. The smile already on his lips stalled... 'Lissa. Hi. I wasn't expecting you.'

Her brows rose. 'Clearly. You look stunned. Rabbit-caught-in-headlights stunned. So who *were* you expecting?' Not antici-pating an answer, she crossed the room, set a bag of Chinese takeout in front of him. 'I was on my way home and remem-bered you said you were working late. Extra Special Fried Rice from the Lotus Pearl. See, I do care about you.'

Its spicy aroma steamed through the plastic carry bag. He wondered if he could extend it to two. 'Thanks, Liss, that's very thoughtful of you and I appreciate it, but I'm not working alone tonight.'

'Didn't you say Pam was off sick? Ah-h-h...' He'd never seen that knowing, womanly expression on his baby sister's face and it threw him for a loop. 'You mean that attractive long-legged brunette in the staffroom lounge making café lattes—for *two*.' Her grin widened—irritatingly so. '*That* kind of working late.'

'No, Liss.' Resisting the temptation to rub the back of his

neck, he pushed out of his seat and grabbed a folder on his bookshelf. 'That's *not* it.'

'I believe you.' She pressed her lips together but the sparkle of humour in her eyes betrayed her. Rising up on tiptoe, she pecked his cheek and murmured, 'Don't work too hard. Or too late.'

Sophie stopped dead outside Jared's door, a café latte in each hand. The sight of the petite but gorgeous Titian-haired female kissing his jaw had her stomach knotting in a strange way. So his almost-flirty conversation this morning had been her imagination. The imagination she'd told him she didn't have.

Her imagination was working just fine now.

As she watched the redhead turn towards the door, Sophie's inner turmoil grew. The girl must be at least a decade younger than him.

And Sophie could cast stones? Hadn't Sophie been years younger than Glen? So young, too young. Too young to know the dangers of falling for the wrong type of man. All she'd wanted was an escape, to feel safe, to belong with someone. To matter. Instead, she'd jumped from one disaster into another.

Before Sophie could analyse her way out of the instant over-reaction, the girl caught sight of her and smiled. 'Hi.' Her aquamarine eyes sparked with feminine curiosity and friendly interest and Sophie couldn't help but like her even though her stomach was tied in double knots.

'I'm sorry,' she murmured. 'I'll come back.'

Jared looked up, bright eyes finding hers. 'No, it's okay, come in. Melissa, this is Sophie.'

Sophie propelled herself towards Jared's desk with a breathy kind of, 'Hi.'

He leaned across and rescued the listing lattes from her stiff fingers. 'Liss brought some fried rice by.'

'That was kind.' Ridiculously relieved for the second time today, Sophie smiled back, her gaze darting between the two but finding no resemblance. Charm and charisma obviously ran in the family, however. 'Pleased to meet you, Melissa.'

'Likewise.' Her voice practically bounced with enthusiasm as she stepped back. 'I'll leave you two to get on with whatever…' With a glance at her brother, she swung her bag onto her shoulder, then smiled at Sophie on her way out. 'Get Jared to bring you over some time.'

'Ah…hmm. Bye for now.'

Was there some sort of conspiracy going on? She could have reiterated that she was temping for the day, that they weren't dating, but she'd been there, said that, this morning. Now hot, flustered and empty-handed, she made an abrupt about-turn as Melissa passed, murmuring, 'I'll just get those reports…'

When she reached her desk, she pressed both palms on its smooth cool surface and took a deep calming breath. Closed her eyes a moment and listened to the muted office sounds as the few staff still remaining closed down computers or chatted outside the elevator bank.

Why was everyone so interested in Jared's social life? More incredible and disturbing were suggestions that she be involved. The fact that he shared a place with his sister surprised her. Surely a man like him would have his own apartment and want to do his own no-doubt-frequent 'entertaining' without a kid sister around, even if said sister was practically an adult?

Sophie didn't care what Pam said, a man with that much sex appeal must have women falling over themselves to get his attention. Pam had meant the workplace, where he was by all accounts legendary for his strict workplace ethics.

And this was the workplace.

Ergo, anything remotely flirty or sexual was off-limits.

Their quick trip to Coolangatta this morning had been a time-out away from the office, Sophie reasoned, hence a little more relaxed. A teensy bit flirty even. But since they'd been back around mid-morning he'd certainly been all business, barely noticing her except to slide some paperwork across her desk to be mailed just before he disappeared around lunchtime for the rest of the day.

Satisfied—and relieved—that the next couple of hours would be no different, she'd lifted the documents and files she'd organised for the evening's session off her desk and turned… to find Jared watching her from the doorway.

And looking anything but business.

The sun had set but the high-rise office was still bathed in the sky's ruddy reflection, painting his skin a swarthy bronze, contrasting with his shirt, which glowed like a white-hot coal. Against the files, her fingers twitched with the itch to stroke his skin and discover if it was as warm and firm as it looked.

As it had felt in her dream.

Sophie inwardly moaned that if she hadn't dreamt about him she wouldn't be having these totally inappropriate thoughts. She prided herself on being a professional. She did *not* gaze at her boss as if she wanted to lick her way up the side of his throat, over his prominent Adam's apple, along his firm afternoon-shadowed jaw to that luscious-looking mouth…

She barely refrained from darting her tongue out to moisten her newly glossed lips courtesy of the quick pit-stop in the Ladies. Which would be a disaster since Jared's gaze seemed to be focused on them with what looked like impatience. Probably waiting for her to explain why she'd been taking so long with the files.

'I do love sunsets, don't you?' she said into the loaded silence and hefted the documents higher against her chest as a kind of barrier.

'Yes. Especially when it's shared with a nice bottle of wine and good company.' He didn't so much as glance towards the window.

'Shall we get started, then?' *No*, she wailed silently as soon as she voiced the words. That came out wrong. Particularly since he was still looking at her lips and she was still drooling over that dusky jaw.

He walked towards her and didn't stop until he was one skinny latte away from her personal space. She didn't move. Just breathed in the scent of his shirt—a day's work mingled with man.

His gaze rose from her lips to meet hers and she realised the one thing she hadn't noticed in her dream was his eyes. That unusual blend of olive and navy. The creases that fanned out from the corners and the long, long eyelashes. How his irises took on the colour of the sunset…or was that gleam she saw there now something else? Speculation? Attraction?

An intimate knowledge of the contents of her diary?

She shivered, caught between desire and dread, but then he reached out, relieved her of the files, thank goodness, because the shiver had spread to her limbs.

If he noticed, he hid it well, suggesting, 'How about that coffee first before it gets cold?'

Rubbing her fingers over the goose-bumps on her upper arms, she murmured, 'Good idea.' The tone in his voice brought everything back to a business level and Sophie forced thoughts of her diary away. 'I hope you like latte—I asked Mimi and she said she thought you did.'

He nodded. 'Anything with caffeine will be welcome around now.'

She followed him into his office, pulled up a chair in front of the paperwork, curled her fingers around her mug for something to grip. To avoid any personal questions or to fill the silence in this strange electrified atmosphere that had sprung up in the past few moments, she asked, 'So…does Melissa have your keen business acumen?'

Jared sat too, drawing his mug close with both hands. 'If she does, she's keeping it to herself. At the moment she's studying design. For her it's all about colour and taking her inspiration from the environment. She's very talented, if I do say so myself.' He smiled. 'A big brother's prerogative.'

Was it? she thought darkly. Hers hadn't thought so. 'Your parents must be very proud of all their children.'

'Our parents are dead.' The dispassionate way he said it sent a chill down her spine.

'Oh…I…' She trailed off, sensing that beneath the utter lack of emotion on his face there was sorrow and anger he no doubt didn't want to share with his temporary employee. 'I'm sorry,' she muttered and immediately could have bitten off her tongue for that tired cliché.

He looked at her as if he'd heard that platitude one time too many, then brought the mug to his lips and swallowed. 'It was a long time ago.'

She should leave it there but she couldn't. She wanted to know more about this man who'd obviously been more than just a brother to his sisters. And now she knew why. He'd taken on a responsibility few other guys would have been willing to do. 'Was…it an accident?'

He shook his head, a faraway look in his eyes. 'Mum died two weeks after Lissa was born. Liss turns eighteen in three weeks.' Then it was as if a winter wind swept over his gaze. 'Dad was killed driving under the influence twelve years ago.' His voice turned brisk and he rose. 'And if we don't eat this rice now the aroma's going to be a distraction.' His quick glance her way told her they had enough distraction to deal with already. 'We can share while we get down to business.'

So he'd changed his mind about a sociable coffee break. Sophie knew it was because the conversation had hit an exposed nerve. She opened the nearest file.

They sipped on their lattes and dipped their forks into the fluffy rice mixture while she brought him up to speed. Rather, he drank and ate while she talked. Which was fine because it helped calm her.

He was a courteous listener, focused on the work spread before them and what she was saying. Putting her at ease. He even asked her opinion on a couple of major proposals he was considering.

Temping wasn't the most satisfying of jobs, but today, thanks to her boss, she felt as if she'd made a contribution. He'd made her feel welcome, and, more importantly, she felt valued as an employee, even if it was temporary.

'We'll call it a day.' He closed the folder they'd been working on.

'Already?' She glanced up, noticing the sky had turned black and the glitter of city lights twinkled below. Where had the time gone?

'It's after eight. That's enough. I'll take it from here.'

She glanced at her watch, incredulous, and gave a half-laugh as she rose. 'You know the old saying about time flying.'

'Thanks for your competent help over the past couple of days.'

Then he smiled. With genuine warmth. And, oh, my, was he drop-dead gorgeous or what? And not only that. How many of the people she'd worked for over the past couple of years had bothered to acknowledge her efforts? She couldn't help but smile back as she met his eyes. 'It's been a pleasure.'

She realised she was still smiling when his eyes turned dark, his pupils expanding till they almost touched that rim of navy. Hotter, spreading warmth over her skin, and she got that he was thinking of pleasure too.

Warning bells clanged in her ears, echoing in the tiny part of her brain that wasn't focused on the pleasure she had no doubt he could provide. She needed to leave. Now. Before something happened that changed…everything. 'If there's nothing else, I'll say goodnight…'

He didn't reply and a shivery sensation swept through her. She stepped away from the chair and through the doorway, then grabbed her bag from the drawer in Pam's desk. With only the reflection off adjacent high-rises, the glow from Jared's office and a security light at one end of the bank of elevators, the entire floor was cloaked in semi-darkness.

The back of her neck prickling—*he hadn't said goodnight so what might that mean?*—she set a brisk pace past the deserted office cubicles. Her pulse rate stepped up and she had to force herself not to break into a run. She was short of breath by the time she pressed the button to summon the lift.

'Wait up, Sophie.' His voice was nowhere near far enough away. 'Where are you parked? I'll walk you to your car.'

She scowled up at the floor numbers as the lift approached from the ground floor with what seemed like agonising slowness. She knew she'd never make sanctuary before he reached her and she said, 'A couple of spaces away from where we parked this morning. I'll be fine,' over her shoulder.

'I'm sure you will but it won't hurt to make sure.'

I wouldn't count on it. The lift doors opened on a cushion of air and she stepped inside. So did Jared. The doors closed, silence and intimacy surrounded them and their eyes met again.

Her feet moved towards the back of the lift, but her gaze remained locked with his and she realised this wasn't just about last night's dream or whether he'd read her dirty diary or not. The glimpse of promised pleasure she saw in his eyes was real—and would have consequences.

She didn't want a man unless he was the kind that faded with dawn. And yet, standing here within Jared's aura and being bathed in his gaze was a naked sensation of heat and desire and imminent surrender, stripping away not only clothing, but denials and reasons.

Beneath her blouse, her skin felt slick, tight. Her blood turned syrupy and throbbed through her veins to a place deep down in her belly and she wanted him with every female cell in her body.

Stupido.

She closed her eyes to lessen the impact. It didn't work

because now her senses focused even more acutely on her body's reaction and her surroundings. She could smell his scent in the confined space and, with all external sound extinguished, she could almost hear him breathing. Worse, she could almost hear him thinking.

'Sophie…'

Her eyes snapped open and were immediately drawn again to his as if there were some kind of force at work. 'Did you press the button?' she asked, and heard her words come out high-pitched and breathless. 'How come the lift's not moving?' And how come she hadn't noticed that? She leaned against the wall. Were they *stuck* in here?

His gaze glittered with something like amusement. One elbow and forearm was casually propped against the lift wall. 'You're not claustrophobic, are you?'

No, they weren't stuck…at least the lift wasn't. 'I don't think so.' Except that the walls seemed to be closing in, or maybe it was Jared's height, the breadth of his shoulders that made it seem that way. And the air…she dragged it in slow and deep… she couldn't seem to find enough.

'Good. Because work's over for the day. In fact your short tour of duty at Sandersons is over.'

Still a little breathless, but a lot relieved, she nodded. *Over. Good.*

His eyes didn't reflect his body's lazy stance. There was alertness and heat in the amusement now, too. Not so good.

He seemed to consider, then spoke slowly. 'So now maybe it's time to confess that I've been thinking about you all day.'

Her heart skipped a beat then pounded so loudly she was sure he'd hear it knocking against her ribs. But did he mean he'd been thinking about her or that cursed diary entry? She glared at him. 'Me? You don't even know me.'

'I know I'd like to.'

'Then you'd learn that I don't get involved with my employers on a personal level.'

'I don't do office flings either. This…thing…whatever it is, is a first for me.' He leaned closer. 'I told you, work's over. We clocked off a good five minutes ago. Correct?'

The warm scent of his skin had her sucking her breath in deeper when she should be exhaling and backing away. 'Yes.' She swallowed. 'But…'

'No "but". I'm attracted to you, Sophie.' He ran a forefinger lightly down the side of her face. 'And the attraction's mutual.'

Blood rushed to the spot on her cheek like iron filings to a magnet. Even when he removed his hand the hot tingly feeling remained and she heard herself asking, '*What* have you been thinking?'

'I've been thinking about how your hair would look if I just unclasped it…'

She couldn't move, could only stand there and let him do it while goose-bumps chased over her body. She had no idea where the clasp vanished to. Was only aware of the weight of her hair tumbling over his arm, then she felt the soothing— *soothing?*—touch of his fingers against the back of her scalp. She didn't feel the least bit soothed and she barely resisted arching against his hand and sighing with pleasure.

She could feel his breath against her face as he leaned closer, could see the faint sheen of damp on his brow, above his lip. And there was no mistaking the arousal smouldering in his eyes.

Her mouth went dry, her heart rate sped up. This wasn't supposed to happen. Never with her boss. And with this man, Jared Sanderson? Not in real life. The paradox was that he might have well and truly brought her undone last night but she'd only met him today.

She was in too deep, too fast. She dragged her gaze from his. 'I should go…' Since he wasn't inclined to shift, she slid a hand past his midriff in search of the control panel behind him.

A subtle but swift move on his part brought her palm into

contact with a hard wall of muscled torso instead. Trapped. Yet his arm was still propping up the wall while the other one played loosely with her hair. He was making no attempt to keep her there and she was shocked and furious with herself for not trying harder to leave. Couldn't she see where this was heading?

She could—that was the problem. And he knew it.

'You've been thinking about me, too.' He caught her hand, held it in a relaxed grip.

'No.'

His thumb whisked over knuckles. 'Admit it, Sophie.'

She made one final, albeit half-hearted, attempt to pull away, but his gaze held hers and he lifted her hand to his chest. His heart thumped strong and deep. 'You've been wondering about our first kiss all day,' he continued in that low seductive tone. 'Like when…' Still massaging the base of her scalp, he leaned in, touched warm, firm lips to hers. *Oh, my.* 'And where…' Heat flowed like honey as he slid the tip of his tongue over her bottom lip. 'And how…'

His mouth moved over hers once more and her lips parted at his gentle coaxing. It perturbed her how easily she let him persuade her, then he released her fingers so that both his hands cupped the back of her skull and she stopped analysing and simply enjoyed the moment.

He slid his tongue against hers. She tasted the sweetness of the coffee they'd drunk, the saltiness of the rice. He made a rough sound that seemed to come from deep in his chest and she sensed the slow smouldering edge of impatience.

Oh, the *'how'*. The slide of his hands over her shoulder blades and all the way down her spine reminding her of her dream. Shifting closer, tucking her against him and, oh…*how* she could feel the hard ridge of his desire.

She leaned into the deepening kiss, wrapping her arms around his neck and momentarily forgetting everything but

Jared. She wanted more. More of that heat, that taste and that rock-hard body against hers. A kiss to build a dream on…

Or a dream to build a kiss on?

No. No. No. She didn't need this complication. She needed to focus on her goals. Her trip. Nothing and no one was going to get in her way. She made one last-ditch effort. 'I need to go,' she snapped out, and reached for the lift panel.

CHAPTER FIVE

'Wait.' Jared moved like lightning, positioning himself in front of the control panel for the second time. Sophie opened her mouth to argue but he spoke over her. 'There's no need to rush off.'

'You don't think?'

Her voice held a slight edge—hysteria or humour? He didn't know her well enough to be sure. She closed her eyes on a soft groan that sounded suspiciously like surrender. His body clenched at the sound and he wondered if she made that noise when she had sex. And just for a moment, looking at her—head tipped back, throat exposed, eyes shut—he could imagine... When she opened them again they were wide and dark gold and...well, simply irresistible.

He reached out to let his fingers glide through the midnight silken waterfall over her shoulders. 'I think you should give it further serious consideration before you decide,' he murmured, bringing her hair to his nose and inhaling the soft herbal fragrance.

Eyes fused with his, she stepped away and he followed until he had her against the elevator wall. He wasn't backing off unless she told him to...and she wasn't saying anything at all. In fact, whatever it was that was flaring to life between them now was as much from her as it was from him.

He caught both her hands, raised them level with her head, and, with her wrists against the wall, he slid his hands over hers. Palm to palm where heat met heat. Still watching her face, he drifted his fingers down. Slowly, so that he could absorb every tiny line and ridge in her palms, then lower still to the rapid beat of her pulse at her wrists.

Enclosing her hands in his, he worked his thumbs deep into her palms—lazy circles, over and over, then slid his fingers between hers, a slow, sinuous rhythm. An erotic imitation of how their bodies would move together when he got her into bed. He saw her gaze widen, her pupils dilate. He leaned close to linger at her mouth, just enough to remind himself of her taste—

'You!' Her whole body stiffening, she reared back. She yanked her hands away, rubbing at her wrists as if they'd been bound. Her eyes flashed hellfire while the air inside the elevator seemed to plummet. 'You—'

'Sophie. Calm down.' He hesitated then reached out but she shrugged him off.

'Don't. Just don't.'

He blew out a slow breath. The hand massage was a dead giveaway. He'd intended it to be because the charade was over. It was time she knew he knew.

'You…*read* it.' Her voice gathered intensity like a low-pressure system crossing the coast. 'Not the first couple of lines, oh, no, you didn't stop when you realised it wasn't meant for you. *You read the whole freaking chapter!*'

'I couldn't put it down. I'm sorry. I should've told you this morning.'

'Yes, you should have.'

'Would it have made a difference?'

'Yes. No.' She shook her head. 'I don't know. How the hell should I know?'

'So…it was a fantasy or a daydream?' he ventured aloud. 'Or a real dream?'

Heat streamed up Sophie's neck. 'Of course it was a real dream! Why on earth would I fantasise about you? I don't even know you.'

Those amused eyes twinkled down at her. 'We seemed to know each other fairly well.' He smiled.

Sophie squirmed. *Thank you so much for pointing that out.* 'I've been recording my dreams for years,' she struggled on. She didn't tell him about her counselling sessions. None of his business. 'They bring forward stuff from our unconscious, help us understand ourselves better. It was nothing to do with *you*, per se.'

He tilted his head and his voice was low when he said, 'What do you think it meant, then?'

She'd done some of her own research. Dream theorists might say she wasn't getting enough love in her life. And they'd be right. That eating in dreams, particularly fruits, like luscious juicy blackberries for instance, were associated with sexuality.

Yep, sexual frustration. Right again. And she was hardly going to tell Mr Sanderson any of that. Nor was she about to tell him she'd never had a dream quite like it. 'I'm at a complete loss,' she said tightly.

'Erotic dream or not, that's some attraction we've got going here. You feel it too. Come on, Sophie, admit it. I'm not letting you out of this lift until you do.'

'Okay. I feel it. It was…good. But it was just a momentary indulgence.'

'Momentary?' When she didn't answer, he said, 'I want to see you again. Away from the office. And believe me, it won't be momentary.'

Her heart battered against her ribcage and the hot flush already invading her body intensified. Oh, the way he said that, the desire in his eyes—for her. But she had to think of practicalities. Nothing was going to persuade her from the goals she'd set for herself. Not even Jared Sanderson. Especially Jared Sanderson because she had a feeling he could change those goalposts to suit himself. 'I'm going overseas, I don't want to start something—'

'Honey, it's already started.'

'That doesn't—'

Her phone's cheerful jangle cut her off. *Salvation.* She pulled the offending item from her bag and answered, turning away from Jared as she did so.

'Sophie, it's Pam. I'm glad I caught you. Can you cover for me for a few more days?'

'Sure.' *Uh-oh.* Definitely *unsure*, but she couldn't tell Pam that right now. She'd need to find a replacement herself. 'You're still not well? Have you seen a doctor?'

'You'll never guess, I've got chicken pox.'

'No way.'

'Discovered the spots a few hours ago, the doctor confirmed it.'

'You poor thing. I'll call in on my way home. Is there anything I can get you?'

'Thanks, but there's no need. I'm going to switch off my phone and sleep. Oh, and I tried phoning Jared before I called you but his mobile's not answering.'

Of course it wasn't. Pam sounded perplexed about that, as if it was completely out of character. And it probably was if he was as dedicated to his work as Pam said.

'Don't worry, I'll let him know.' She rubbed at her temple. 'I'll talk to you tomorrow. Ring me if you need anything, no matter what time. Day or night.'

Sophie disconnected but remained facing the back of the lift. She didn't want the sight of Jared distracting her any more than she wanted to be the one who'd distracted him. The memory of the past few minutes burned in her blood. Her lips still tingled with his taste. Her entire body felt as if it were smouldering. How could she possibly cover for Pam now? But that extra income would have come in so handy.

Hearing the tightness in her voice as she disconnected, Jared touched Sophie's shoulder. 'What's wrong? Anything I can do?' None of his business, but he had to ask. He knew what it was like to deal with family crises.

'That was Pam.' Slipping the phone in her bag, she turned, her expression taut, shoulders rigid.

'And…?' he prompted when she just stared at him as if he'd turned into some kind of monster.

'She's got chicken pox.'

'*Chicken pox?* Do adults even catch chicken pox?'

'They can. Sometimes.'

Before he'd finished saying, 'That's unfortunate,' his mind was already leaping ahead. Sophie. At his beck and call for a week…but not in his bed as he'd anticipated. He didn't fool around with his staff.

'Pam tried to contact you just now,' she continued in a voice devoid of that husky passion he'd heard earlier. 'I told her I'd let her know.' She hesitated before saying, 'Under the circumstances I'll arrange for someone to cover for her.'

'No. I want you.' His body, already pumped, hardened further. He fought it down. *Hang on a damn minute.* They were talking business hours here. 'I need a PA and you need the work.' When she didn't reply he pressed on. 'Couldn't you use the extra spending money?'

'Yes, but—'

'So I'll see you here bright and early in the morning. Sophie, you're a professional, you can do it. Think of London. That side trip to Paris.'

'I wasn't planning a side trip to Paris.'

'Everyone plans a side trip to Paris.'

'Not me.' She chewed her lip a moment. 'I want to see Rome. And maybe Florence.' Stepping sideways, she stabbed the elevator button…and this time he let her.

The quiet click of gears was the only sound in the rapidly descending lift but the residual crackle of sexual energy sparking off the walls was deafening.

'Okay…' she murmured finally. 'We'll give it a try.'

He watched her refusing to look at him. It wouldn't work if they didn't talk about it. 'You don't want to resolve this unfinished business first?'

'There's nothing to resolve,' she said, tight-lipped. 'As for unfinished, as of now, what just happened here didn't happen. And I'd like my hair clasp back, please.'

He withdrew the tortoiseshell clasp from his pocket, handed it to her. 'Your idea's not going to work, you know.'

She shot him a look while she twisted her hair into a rope, jammed it haphazardly into the clasp. 'It will. I'm your employee. Everything changes. We've acknowledged…the whatever it is. Now we can ignore it and—'

'It'll go away?'

'Exactly.'

They exited the lift. The front doors opened and they stepped out into a muggy evening swamped with humidity and the *brzzz* of night insects.

'You really think so?'

'I *know* so.'

'I like your optimism.'

She turned left and headed for her car, her heels clicking a brisk rhythm on the pavement. 'What's more, I have every confidence in your ability to do the same.' She keyed the remote and a dark-coloured hatch's lights winked. 'We're both professionals.'

Professional. With the star-spattered sky stretched over a calm ocean and a woman he'd just been enjoying getting up close and personal with beside him, professional was as far from Jared's mind as that distant Pacific horizon.

She came to an abrupt stop beside her car, yanked open the door and tossed her bag across the seat all in rapid succession. 'Goodnight.'

Strands of hair she hadn't managed to contain in her clasp moved in the breeze. She still had that just kissed look. Plump lips, overbright eyes, breathing a little too fast.

The salty tropical evening was made for loving and for once he didn't want professional. If she'd been a date, he'd have been working that top buttonhole in her blouse right now. Hell no, he'd have had her naked already and moaning for more—after all, he knew what she liked, didn't he?

He fisted his hands in his pockets. *Cool it.* 'Okay. We'll try it your way.' He schooled his voice to neutral. 'So goodnight, Sophie, and thanks for working back, I appreciate it. Is that friendly-formal enough for you?'

She nodded once. It amused him to note that she actually looked disappointed he hadn't pushed his luck and kissed her again. Not that she'd want him to know he'd noticed. Her slim dark brows pulled down as she climbed into the car. 'You're welcome. Goodnight.'

'See you in the morning.' He shut her car door and watched till she pulled out of the car park. He let her go because she was still stinging with the knowledge that he'd read her dream. But he didn't care how determined she was to deny their attraction, tomorrow after hours they were going to talk about it. And then he'd inform her that his business plans for Noosa next week were already set and they included his PA.

Sophie checked the rear-vision mirror to ensure Jared wasn't following her, then pulled over to the side of the road. She switched off the ignition, let her head fall back on the seat and closed her eyes. *Oh. My. God.*

She blew out a shuddering breath. She'd managed to keep it together, but now that she could fall apart in private her whole body trembled. Darts of what felt like electric shocks tingled through her limbs and over her skin.

He'd made love to her hands exactly the way she'd told him to in her dream. The only difference with tonight's scenario was that they hadn't used her Secret Sensation moisturiser or done it naked and horizontal on some fluffy mat that didn't exist—at least it didn't in her house.

And he'd know that too.

She slammed her palms over and over against her temples. He'd read her diary entry. He'd known, damn him, and he'd said nothing all day. He'd probably watched her when she wasn't looking and imagined all the things she'd written... She could quite easily kill him and with no conscience at all. In fact, when she pulled herself together again she still might.

He kissed like a dream.

And, oh, that was *so-o-o* not funny. She sighed, remembering the luscious feel of his lips on hers, how she'd lost all willpower, wound her arms around his neck and practically sucked his face off.

He'd let her make a complete fool of herself. No, she'd done that on her own by sending the wrong email. She should have come clean with him first thing this morning and got it out of the way. Instead of hoping he hadn't read it. Of course he'd have read it. What normal red-blooded guy in his sexual prime would stop at the first couple of lines?

Since he'd asked her to stay on and she'd agreed, changing her mind and phoning the office in the morning wasn't an option. Her pride wouldn't allow it and an extra week's pay would be more than welcome. She considered herself a responsible employee. She didn't let people down, particularly Pam, the one person who'd been there for Sophie when she'd needed support.

But this thing with Pam's boss couldn't continue. It would affect their working relationship and her ability to do her job. Tomorrow she'd inform Jared she'd do her best to cover for Pam but that outside office hours she wanted nothing whatsoever to do with him.

After a practically sleepless but mercifully dream-free night of trying not to think of the mess her life had become, Sophie spent the morning filing and typing up reports that had been accumulating in Pam's inbox. She'd beaten Jared to the office by ten minutes, organised his agenda for the day and greeted him all cool, smooth politeness on his arrival. He'd been no less courteous, with hardly more than a flicker in his eye to remind her of last night.

But that single flicker was the killer.

It was more than hot enough to set her cheeks aglow and remind her that beyond these walls she wasn't going to get involved with him. She'd needed to excuse herself and make a dash to the bathroom to pat cold water on her face with a tissue and think calming thoughts.

Jared was in the town centre somewhere busy with appointments all morning and this afternoon he was driving into the Gold Coast Hinterland. Good. He hadn't asked her to come with him. Even better. Instead, he'd left her with a further list of proposals and phone calls to follow up. *Those* she could manage.

Then just before midday the helium balloons arrived. A dozen heart-shaped pink foil balloons tied to a small pink and white striped box.

'This can't be right,' Sophie told the uniformed delivery girl who was touting the arrangement in front of her desk.

'I was told to bring them over here.' She glanced in Mimi's direction, shrugged, then set them on Sophie's desk with a smile. 'Have a nice day.'

'And you.' Sophie's smile felt brittle and, inside, her anger built like a tropical storm. Ignoring the attached envelope, she picked up the whole thing, carried it into Jared's office and dumped it in front of his computer screen.

She scowled, its pretty, cheerful presence only infuriating her further. After his assurance to the contrary, how *dare* he bring their attraction and what had happened between them last night into office hours? And so publicly. She couldn't believe it.

And yet…something deep down, something she'd almost

forgotten how to feel, let alone respond to, fluttered around the region of her heart.

She shoved it down deeper. A solitary lunch in the fresh air would be a timely and welcome distraction so she took her sandwiches to the beach, a few minutes' walk away.

She'd been back at her desk twenty minutes when she heard Jared's voice. He was too far away for her to hear what he was saying but the relaxed delivery in those deep sexy tones sent her pulse into overdrive.

Suddenly she wished she hadn't been so hasty with the balloons and, since she'd not read the note, she didn't know what to accuse him of... She pushed out of her chair. If she could just duck back into his office and undo...

She swore inwardly. Too late, he was coming this way. With his sister. Her heart pounding, she grabbed a file she'd set aside to take down to Accounting on the floor below. Now seemed like a good time...

'Sophie.' He slowed as he passed her desk on his way to his office. 'Any problems this morning?' The expression in his eyes told her he wasn't only referring to computer glitches and client complaints.

'No.'

The denial sounded like a sharpened icicle, and he blinked in surprise. So she smiled—for Melissa's benefit. 'Everything's fine.'

Jared paused, then must have decided whatever he was going to say could wait, nodded and kept walking.

Sophie turned to his sister, glad of an excuse to look away. 'Hello, Melissa.'

'Hi. You must think I have nothing better to do than hang around my brother.' She grinned. 'I assure you nothing's further from the truth. But he's giving me a lift back to uni after we've been to the hospital.'

'Right, let's go.' Jared reappeared, briefcase in one hand, balloons in the other.

'Oh, they're gorgeous, she'll love them.' Melissa reached out and ran a hand over the foil ribbons.

Sophie stared. Uh-huh. *R-i-g-h-t...* The balloons were for the new arrival. How stupid and naïve of her to presume and she'd presumed so wrongly. She wished they'd leave now so that she could have her third—or was it her fourth?—hysterical breakdown.

But Melissa was in no hurry. 'I want to show Sophie the baby bracelet first. We're going to put it in the little box with the balloons.'

Jared's phone buzzed. He muttered, 'Liss, Sophie looks like she's busy,' as he pulled it from his pocket.

'It'll only take a minute.' Melissa pulled a little packet from her bag, opened it and poured the contents into Sophie's palm. 'Isn't it precious?'

Sophie stared at the delicate gold links, the tiny heart clasp with Arabella's name engraved on it. Beautiful. But not nearly as precious as the tiny new life it was named for.

'It's the sweetest thing,' she agreed, forcing a smile and returning the bracelet to Melissa. 'Crystal will love it and so will Arabella when she's old enough.'

Jared was still talking as he walked back into his office and closed the door. Sophie grabbed the opportunity to escape further face-to-face contact and waved her folder. 'If you'll excuse me, I was just on my way down to Accounts...enjoy your visit to the hospital.'

She walked swiftly towards the elevators, then changed her mind and veered towards the stairs. She didn't want to have to wait for the lift and risk sharing it with them, especially with last night's memories still steaming up the walls.

In Accounts she took her time delivering the folder. Introducing herself to George, the balding fifty-something head honcho. Waiting while he fumbled through the mess on his desk for a report to take upstairs to Jared. Long enough to give Jared and Melissa time to leave the building. But in case they hadn't, she decided returning the way she'd come was the safest option.

CHAPTER SIX

TEN minutes later Jared disconnected and exited his office to find Lissa balanced on the corner of Sophie's desk, fiddling with the balloon ties. Sophie was nowhere to be seen.

He must have frowned because Lissa smiled as if she knew something she shouldn't and said, 'She went downstairs,' then glanced at her watch. 'We need to—'

'Did she say anything to you?' he demanded before he could rein in his impatience. Professional communication with his PA was key and Sophie was avoiding him.

Lissa raised her brows. 'Like what? Come to think of it, she did look kind of flustered. Did you upset her?'

'No. Wait in the car.' He tossed her the keys and headed for the elevator.

'She took the stairs,' he heard Lissa call behind him. 'Don't be long, I've got a class…'

The smell of cool musty concrete invaded his nostrils as he yanked open the door to the stairwell. It swung shut with a hollow boom, cutting off Lissa's voice.

He started down, taking the steps two at a time. He needed an assistant who could put personal issues aside during office hours and work with him. He didn't have time for this game of denial she seemed to be playing.

He heard the door on the floor below open, close. Peering over the railing, he saw Sophie starting up. Slowly, as if she didn't have an afternoon's work awaiting her.

As if she was making sure he'd left before she made her reappearance.

A file she was holding slipped and she grabbed at it, giving him a peek of cleavage. Smooth, dusky, *inviting* cleavage. He ran a tongue over his teeth. She wore a conservative dress the colour of watermelon. Square neckline, straight skirt, wide emerald-green belt.

His body hardened as he remembered last night. The taste of her skin, her sexy little moan as he'd tucked her against him. The way her eyes had clashed with his when she'd felt his erection. She'd been all-the-way with him. Willing, wanting, desperate. Until Pam had rung.

She was still interested. If he'd found another temp he could have been seeing Sophie socially this evening. He'd not been thinking straight when he'd talked her into staying on as his PA. He'd just wanted to see her again and the sooner, the better.

Okay, she was a current employee, but not for long. A few days, then nothing was stopping them acting on that attraction for however long it lasted. She was off overseas indefinitely in a matter of weeks, which suited him fine—he was nowhere near ready for anything long term. And obviously she didn't want serious either at this point.

Perfect. Well, almost.

So they were going to clear this up. Now. As he descended she glanced up and caught sight of him. He watched the dismay cross her gaze. Watched her stop and try to compose herself.

'Sophie.'

'Jared.' She jiggled the folders she held tighter against her bosom. 'Do you want to go over these figures from George before I file them?'

'No. That's what I pay you for.' He stopped two steps above her, then sat down on the concrete so that they were eye to eye. 'Last night you said you were a professional.'

Her eyes widened. 'And I am.'

'You're avoiding me.'

'No. I'm busy.' Then her gaze turned worried. 'Oh. Since you were on your way out I figured I'd—'

'I don't have time for this, Sophie, and nor do you. We need to do something about it.' He wanted to touch her so badly he had to fist his hands at his sides. 'Whatever you're doing tonight, cancel it.'

'I can't. Not tonight.'

He narrowed his eyes while trying to read hers. 'Can't or won't?'

'I'm spending the night with Pam.' Her lips firmed and her eyes flashed a defiant topaz. 'She's family to me and she's ill and on her own. So call me unprofessional or sack me on the spot but an understanding boss knows which comes first.'

Yes, he knew. He had to admire her for standing up for herself. 'Okay.' Rising and stepping down to her level, he breathed out his frustration. Slowly. 'Tomorrow night, then.'

She took her time responding, as if trying to come up with another excuse. He decided to let her off the hook for now and said, 'Listen, why don't you finish here early today since you worked back last night? Buy some flowers from the staff at the florist around the corner on your way. You'd know what Pam likes. Put it on my business account.'

Her tensed shoulders softened. 'Okay. Thanks. Pam'll love that.' A smile lit up her whole face and reflected in her gold-flecked eyes. It brought a glow to the moment. It made him think of the sun dancing on a sapphire sea. It made him forget he was her boss and this was his place of work.

'Summer,' he murmured. Heat. Bared, bronzed bodies. Playtime and passion. He wanted it all with Sophie Buchanan.

The images his mind seemed determined to conjure up both startled and aroused. He breathed in sharply and his nostrils filled with her familiar fresh scent. Her smile faded as they continued to stare at each other. His heart pounded like a fist on a drum. Her shoulders tensed up again and she gripped the metal banister with her free hand, the other clutching at the files.

'Hey...' Seriously aiming for detached, he grinned, then... somehow...his thumb was sliding along her lower lip. 'Relax, I'm not going to ravish you on the stairwell no matter how hard you beg.'

She didn't smile or move a muscle, didn't react in any way. A block of wood. His inappropriate touch and humour drained away, leaving him feeling confused, unsteady and...damn *exposed*... What the hell was wrong with him? With his body already rock hard, he shifted closer, desperate for one taste of that generous mouth, just one...

She didn't move away. She didn't resist as he leaned in and the instant their lips met her whole being seemed to sigh with satisfaction. He knew because he felt the same way. Her mouth, so warm, so soft, so rich. So right. His body tightened further.

The sound of the upstairs door opening echoed in the stairwell. He reacted instantly. *What in hell was he doing?* This wasn't *so right*, this was *all wrong*. His hands instinctively rose to Sophie's shoulders—to steady her, that was all—but she shot backwards, still grasping the files, wide eyes flashing with accusation.

'Jared?' an impatient voice called. 'Are you down there? Some of us haven't got all day...'

'Be there in a jiff, Liss.' His voice reverberated off the walls.

He heard a strangled sound coming from Sophie, who was shooting upwards like a rocket and already a few stairs above him. She turned, looked down on him and whispered fiercely, 'That's what happens when you don't stick to the rules.'

He was uncomfortably aware of the tent in his trousers. Sophie would be too. And Melissa, if she noticed. And Melissa would be bound to notice. He ground his teeth. *Sisters*. He threw out a hand, snapped his fingers. 'Give me the files, Sophie.'

She passed them down to him with…was that a hint of smoky humour mingled with the agitation in her eyes? 'I'll let Melissa know you'll be right along,' she said, and resumed her ascent.

'Tell her I'll meet her in the car park. And check the agenda for next Wednesday and familiarise yourself with the details,' he informed her retreating back, trying to get some sort of business rapport going between them again.

'Next Wednesday?'

'I've left you an email.'

'I'll get right on it.'

The door above swung shut. He drew in a ragged breath and tried to bring his wayward body under some sort of control. He couldn't believe what he'd just done. During office hours. With his PA, for pity's sake. What an ass.

His professional self had never done anything remotely like it. Never been tempted. Sophie Buchanan was the first. The one-off.

When he'd kissed her last night he'd not anticipated she'd still be his PA today. He reassured himself that in less than a month everything would be back to normal.

Who was he kidding? He shook his head as he made his way upstairs. Somehow he doubted anything would be the same, ever again.

Noosa? They were going to Noosa. Sophie stared at the email Jared had forwarded moments ago while she'd been downstairs. Her and him, together for the three-hour journey past Brisbane and on to the northern Sunshine Coast. And staying at some fancy address on the Noosa River. Alone.

No way.

She reached for the office phone, but before she could make a connection it buzzed. To curb her impatience she fixed a smile in place. 'Sanderson Property Investments, Sophie Buchanan speaking, how may I help you?'

'Miz Buchanan.' Jared's voice. With not a hint of the husky heat it had exuded moments ago. Just deep and calm like a high mountain lake.

Unlike her. Her pulse, which had barely settled, raced again. He'd kissed her senseless and just like that, now he was being all business? She heard a car's horn in the background. Right, of course he was all business because he was in the car with Melissa, who was no doubt listening in on every word. *Now who's playing games?*

'*Mr* Sanderson.' She leaned back in her chair, tapping her fingernails on the desk and studying the photo of Noosa's riverside luxury home on her computer screen. 'What can I do for you?'

Should have rephrased that. A shiver shimmied down her spine and she swore that amazing sexual tension they seemed to have between them spun through the air, as if he were standing right behind her. Leaning down, his breath hot against her ear—

'You've read the email, I presume?'

She jolted upright. 'Yes.' Brief hiatus where neither spoke. Did he expect her to back out now? Moreover, did she *want* to back out now? The refusal on the tip of her tongue melted away. 'I'll be ready,' she said.

'Excellent.'

No way could she interpret the nuance of that single word.

'We've a busy schedule ahead of us,' he continued, 'and I want to familiarise you with a few details before we leave on Wednesday. I'll be in Brisbane on Monday and Tuesday, so we'll discuss it over dinner tomorrow evening.'

She opened her mouth to argue, closed it. So it was a business dinner now. How cunning. And when he put it that way how could she refuse? 'Very well. Restaurants…' She flipped through Pam's list on the desk. 'Do you have a preference?'

'I'll make the reservations this time. We'll make it seven, I'll pick you up on the way.'

Nuh-uh, that sounded too much like a date and the panicky feeling fluttered back. 'I—'

'Until tomorrow, then. Bye for now.'

The line went dead.

'Fill me in on the latest lunchroom gossip,' Pam said while they ate the home-made chicken soup and hot crusty bread Sophie had brought upstairs.

Pam was a brunette with short bouncy hair, abundant curves and dark expressive eyes. Right now those eyes begged for news from the outside.

'I'm just the temp, remember. I'm not privy to gossip.'

'But you must have heard something—any sordid little tidbit that'll brighten up my miserable, itchy and scratch-filled day will do.'

'Oh, you poor thing.' Sophie looked at her blister-covered friend across the table and almost felt itchy herself. 'Are you sure there's not anything I can get you?'

'Thanks, but I'm fully medicated for the moment. Especially with the gorgeous flowers you brought. Jared really is a darling.' She smiled at the bunch of yellow roses on the coffee table. 'Come on, Sophie.'

She wanted to get this thing with Jared out in the open with someone and Pam was the only person she was close enough and trusted enough to confide in. 'Are you sure you're up to hearing it? You don't need to go and relieve that itching some more in a cool cornflower bath?'

Pam's eyes brightened considerably. 'You *have* heard something. Out with it. Now.'

'Okay, but don't blame me if your itch turns feral. It may take a while and you have to promise not to tell.'

Leaning her elbows on the table, Pam settled in. 'Promise.'

'It started two nights ago when I emailed your report to Jared, only it wasn't your report that I emailed...'

When Sophie had finished, Pam sat back and stared at her. 'Oh, *cringe*... You're genuine. If I hadn't heard it from you I'd never have believed it.'

'I can hardly believe it myself. And yeah, the cringe factor for this particular blunder surpasses all previous records.'

'Agreed.' Pam's slow smile had a hint of wicked humour about it. 'You and Jared together. It's kind of...I'm not sure yet, let me think on it.'

'Not too deeply, please.' Sophie felt her cheeks heat and dared herself to hold Pam's gaze. 'And let me point out we're not *together* together.'

But after that moment on the stairs this afternoon... When he'd touched her lips with that very tanned, very sexy and no doubt very experienced thumb, it had been all she could do not to open her mouth and take it inside. To wrap her tongue around it and taste him.

Then he'd swooped in and kissed her. He'd tasted rich, dark, hot. But it hadn't been long enough. Not nearly long enough. She pressed her lips together. Hard.

And now...now there was next Wednesday... *Business* trip, she reminded herself.

'There's never been a whiff of scandal around Jared.' Pam interrupted Sophie's thoughts. 'But if they see you the way you are now...all pink and flustered-looking...I wonder who'll be the first to start the rumour mill?'

Sophie glared at her. 'Not you. You promised.'

Pam made a zipping movement with her thumb and forefinger. 'My lips are sealed.'

'Tell me what I should know about this upcoming trip to Noosa. I only found out about it this afternoon. By *email*.' The funny feeling she'd got in her stomach back at the office unfurled again and started to flap.

'We were going to Noosa to consult with a few clients and look at property,' Pam said.

'*And* staying overnight,' Sophie continued.

'Two nights actually.' Pam smiled as if they were co-conspirators in a secret, and that funny sensation flapped some more.

'What if I don't want to go?'

'Are you seriously thinking of refusing?'

'I—'

'Because if you are, you'd better organise someone else pronto.' Pam sounded surprisingly aggrieved. 'This trip's important to Jared.' She stared hard at Sophie. 'I know I go on about him but, honestly, he's one of the good guys. Think of England. Spending money, Soph.'

Rome, Florence. The Colosseum. Michelangelo's David. 'Thinking, thinking. Still doesn't make it a good idea.'

Sophie realised she wasn't focusing on the professional aspect. She was temping for Pam and Pam had wangled this job for her instead of going through the agency as she was supposed to. She couldn't let her down. 'Just my thoughts spinning, Pam. Of course I'm going.'

Pam's expression relaxed. 'Don't worry, the accommodation's a luxury waterfront home on Noosa River. Five bedrooms, four bathrooms, spa, pool.'

'I've been looking at the info.'

'So you'll know there's plenty of room to stay out of each other's way if that's what you want… Is that what you want, Sophie?'

Sophie evaded the question with one of her own. 'Why not a couple of rooms in a hotel?'

'Because Jared wants to refurbish a place here in Surfers that he's purchased for himself. He saw this one available for short-term rent on the net and liked some of the ideas. And it makes a change from hotels. Lighten up, work might actually be fun for a change. For both of you.'

Oh, Sophie had no doubts about that. None at all. But when they came back she could see the word *Complication* looming on the horizon, even if Pam was back at work by then. 'Okay, tell me more. What's he like out of office hours?'

Pam studied her through very perceptive eyes. Too perceptive. 'He's turned up at staff functions with gorgeous sophisticates—always blonde—but never the same one twice. Does that answer your question?'

Sophie shrugged as if it didn't matter. 'I reckon so.' It *didn't* matter, she told herself. She frowned, annoyed. It was no concern of hers how many women he had. Then she remembered Jared's words. *A good thing is only a good thing for as long as you enjoy it.* 'So he's commitment phobic.'

Pam pursed her lips. 'I'd say it's more like work-focused.'

Sophie *hmphed*. She'd reserve judgment on that for now.

'Career and family are his life,' Pam went on. 'He fought for and won guardianship of Crystal and Melissa when he was only eighteen. That was twelve years ago and he's done a brilliant job all while expanding a now very lucrative and successful business.'

Oh. Sophie tried not to be impressed with his dedication and commitment. It didn't extend to his relationships with the opposite sex. Again she tried not to compare him with her ex-husband but she couldn't help it. Glen had loved women. Lots of women.

All behind Sophie's back.

And it seemed both men preferred blondes.

Superficial beings, men. A timely reminder and one she intended keeping uppermost in her mind for the next few days. Weeks. And even when she boarded that big shiny jet and headed for the other side of the world she would remember.

Superficial suited her purposes too. Superficial was safe.

She thought about that later, lying in bed and staring at the ceiling while the tropical breeze did nothing to cool her overheated body. Overheated because she couldn't stop thinking about Jared. In that *superficial* way.

He made her hot. From his tanned skin and toned body to the way he looked at her with those intense eyes the colour of smouldering olive leaves.

Then there were his lips. Firm and full and fabulous. The way he'd used them to kiss her. Talk about weapons of mass seduction. Her temperature rose another degree just thinking about it. She wanted those lips against hers again. She wanted them on other parts of her body—the way they'd worshipped her in her dream.

Rolling over, she squeezed her pillow and bunched it beneath her head. Why was this happening *now* when she was leaving Australia indefinitely?

She'd never been kissed by a man like Jared, certainly never involved with one. It was an all-new experience. A cocktail of power and authority with a twist of devilish wit and charm, to be served hot in a dark grey suit. Enticing, irresistible.

Possibly lethal.

But even though Pam the PA certified him all work and no play, Sophie knew Pam her friend considered him the quintessential good bloke.

Not so superficial.

Not so safe after all.

CHAPTER SEVEN

THE workload Jared gave Sophie on Friday was so heavy she barely had time to go to the Ladies, let alone think of him in any other way than her slave-driver boss.

She didn't have time to think of him at all actually. She worked her butt off all morning without a coffee break, and by lunch she'd cleared most of the paperwork. She stretched in her chair, wiggled her fingers, satisfied with her efforts, then reached beneath her desk and pulled out her lunch box.

'These need filing, please.'

Jared dumped another pile of manila folders on her desk. She realised he'd hardly have noticed if Pam had come back early and was sitting in this chair instead of Sophie.

'Right away.' She watched him not looking at her as he walked past.

He turned back just when she thought he wasn't going to acknowledge her in any way and said, 'And see if you can dig up the hard copy of the works schedule for the Carson Richardson project from last month, ASAP, client wants alterations as of yesterday.'

Resigned, Sophie slid her lunch box back into her bag. 'I'll get right on it.'

He checked his watch. 'I'll be back at two, if you can have it ready for me by then.'

* * *

'For heaven's sake, Sophie, you haven't stopped all morning,' Mimi said at one-thirty. 'You *are* permitted a lunch break. Take one.'

She did. She ate her honey and walnut sandwiches in the lunchroom and washed it down with a coffee all in under ten minutes. No way was she going to let Jared see that she wasn't up to the job. She could handle anything he threw at her. In fact, she wondered if he was testing her, just to see how she performed under pressure. Why, she had no idea. It wasn't as if she'd be a regular here.

The rest of the day kept up the same frenetic pace. In one way it was good because it took her mind off the man and the evening ahead. Mostly.

The business dinner, she reminded herself as she responded to an email enquiry.

Five-thirty rolled by. Five forty-five. Sophie had plenty of work still to keep her busy but she really needed to know the details for tonight. Since he hadn't mentioned it again, neither had she.

Jared and a client were still in his office. With the door closed. The ebb and flow of a tense-sounding conversation warned her it wasn't a good time to interrupt. Was she to assume the arrangement still stood?

The door opened and both men walked out.

'Sophie. What are you still doing here? It's almost six.'

'I needed to finalise a few details.' *Like where to meet you tonight?* But she could hardly ask that in front of a client and give the impression it was business. Not with the flush she could already feel creeping up her neck.

She smiled blandly at his client, then busied herself tidying her desk. 'I'm just on my way home now.' Not that Jared heard; he was already walking away. She clicked off the screen and closed down the computer.

A moment later, Jared returned from seeing the guy to the elevator. 'You're still here.'

'You noticed,' she said with asperity and immediately regretted it. She reached for her bag. It was the sort of jealous female response you might give a lover and wasn't what she'd meant, in addition to being totally inappropriate in the workplace.

He stared at her a full ten seconds with those intense green eyes. She had him speechless. A first. Then he said, 'You're still on for tonight, I hope,' and something in his gaze sharpened.

She felt its effects right down to her toes. 'Why wouldn't I be?'

'So you're one of those quick dressers, are you? That'll be a first.'

'Not particularly,' she said, trying for nonchalant, but that flick of his eyes over her body as he'd spoken had felt like a flame thrower. 'You haven't told me where to meet you.'

'I told you yesterday I'm picking you up at seven.' The tone of command with a dash of impatience.

'I said I'd meet you there…wherever.'

'No. You didn't.'

He was right, she realised. He'd cut her off when she'd tried to ask. With a little resigned inward sigh, she slung her bag over her shoulder. She didn't have time to argue and she knew she wouldn't win this one. She also knew it wasn't all business, so she asked, 'What's the dress code for this place you've chosen?'

'How does casually elegant sound?'

'Fine.'

'Pacific Gold apartments…?'

'Unit 213.'

'Make it seven-fifteen.'

Humour snuck in and she arched a brow. 'We agreed on seven. You saying you can't be ready in fifty-five minutes?'

He didn't reply but his eyes flashed a challenge.

She shook her head once. 'Seven o'clock.' She turned away quick smart and headed towards the lift, praying, praying, he didn't follow. She simply couldn't handle another trip in the elevator with him right now.

Jared drove home only a touch above the speed limit and jumped in the shower. He didn't have time to think about the tight sensation in his chest, nor to acknowledge the sense of anticipation he hadn't felt since his teenage years. Which was just as well.

Moments later he ran his fingers through his damp hair. Quick shave, splash of subtle cologne at the last minute. He threw on dark chinos and an open-necked oatmeal linen shirt. No tie. *Casual* business dinner. One that might lead to a more relaxed after-dinner coffee somewhere?

He was walking to the front door at the same time as Melissa, also dressed for a night out.

'Wow.' Looking him up and down, she sniffed the air. 'Is that a new cologne?'

'You and Crystal gave it to me last Christmas.' He just hadn't had an occasion to wear it. 'And it's a business dinner, Liss.'

'I certainly hope so—I heard you arrange it in the car. You wouldn't win any dates with that austere approach…' She studied him some more, met his eyes with a cryptic look. 'You don't *look* business… Are you going to be late home?'

'I don't know, Liss,' he said, annoyed and running late. She was asking *him* that question? 'Why?'

'Just letting you know I'll be out late too,' she said, walking to the door ahead of him. 'I'm meeting friends for burgers then we're going clubbing later.'

'Don't get into a vehicle with anyone who's been drinking.'

He was checking for his wallet but he could almost see her eyes rolling up as she walked down the garden path when he heard, 'No, Daddy.'

* * *

He made it to the front door of Sophie's apartment with two minutes to spare.

The door opened as he was about to knock and he was looking straight into those eyes, touched with humour now. 'What took you so long?' she said.

'No points for being early?'

Her warm brandy eyes weren't the only things attracting his attention. His gaze dipped. She was wearing a slim white knee-length dress. A complicated series of straps pulled the bodice into a bunch of fabric just below her collarbone and tied behind her neck, leaving her shoulders bare. Stunning smooth shoulders that gleamed like honey in the amber light behind her.

So she hadn't gone with strictly business either.

Half-moon earrings the colour of limes dangled on gold thread. She wore a matching bracelet. She reminded him of a tropical milkshake cocktail, long and cool and inviting. Too inviting. He wished they could just dine in. On each other.

'I'll grab a jacket.' She hesitated before asking, 'Do you want to come in for a moment?'

Come in? His groin tightened. *More than you know and for a lot longer than a minute.* He cleared his throat. 'Maybe later.'

She disappeared while he counted the various species of tropical flora on the other side of the balcony that formed a courtyard within the apartment block, and thought about penguins and Antarctica and ice-cold beer.

When she pulled the door closed, mercifully he had himself pretty much under control. 'I hope you like seafood.'

'Love it.' She led the way. They took the stairs down. Three flights. 'I try to keep fit.'

She didn't need to explain; it was obvious the elevator was a problem for her. He thought of telling her so. It would be ridiculous if they couldn't even manage an elevator together, but he also wanted to make it to the restaurant with a dinner partner. He wanted her at ease with him. It was vital to have her comfortable in their working relationship. Or any kind of relationship.

The journey took ten minutes. On the way Jared stuck to the usual and asked about her working day. They pulled up outside Enzo's Seafood and Grill and were shown to a corner table overlooking the beach where a few tiny lights winked on the dark strip of ocean.

With the fine weather this evening, the windows had been removed, allowing the balmy tropical evening in and giving the impression they were outside. On the decking a string of party lights and a couple of flaring bamboo torches provided a warm ambience.

After they'd ordered, for the first time all day, Sophie forced herself to relax. To enjoy the experience of dining with a gorgeous man at a classy restaurant and converse on a variety of non-threatening topics. The latest in local entertainment, the real estate market. The pros and cons of living in a high-profile tourist destination.

The champagne he'd ordered was perfection—cold and fruity and fizzy. Her prawn and avocado cocktail tasted fresh and sweet. On the table, the tiny tea light inside its ruby glass cube seemed to draw them closer. Way too intimate for a business dinner but *business* wasn't what this was about. Had never been what this was about. She knew it. He knew it.

While she waited for him to initiate the discussion on the supposed reason they were here, she took another sip of wine and let the bubbles tickle her nostrils and dance on her tongue. She'd not seen Jared in anything other than business attire and this more relaxed Jared was no less stunning.

He'd taken the short time he'd had to shave and to splash on something that made her want to lean forward and breathe him in. But she wouldn't want to stop at breathing… To avoid the temptation, she reached for her napkin, pressed it to her lips and leaned back.

'Good evening, Jared.' A good-looking Italian appeared at their table. Black hair and eyes, and a roguish smile, which was currently directed at Sophie. 'And to your lovely dinner companion tonight.'

Jared grinned at him then at Sophie. 'Enzo. I'd like you to meet Sophie Buchanan. She's filling in for my PA for a few days.' He turned to Sophie. 'Enzo's Rico's brother.'

'Ah, yes, the best fish and chips in Coolangatta. I remember. Pleased to meet you, Enzo.'

He smiled at her again, all smooth Italian charisma. 'We're very busy tonight or I'd stay and chat. Charmed to meet you, Sophie. Come back another time, meanwhile have a pleasant evening.'

Sophie smiled back. 'Thank you.'

They'd decided on a shared seafood platter; a variety of oysters, salt and pepper calamari, grilled prawns and tempura garfish, served with a crisp rocket salad drizzled with a lemon olive oil dressing.

Conversation ceased while Sophie, who'd eaten nothing all day but her sandwich several hours ago, savoured every delicious mouthful and made each one count. How often did she get to eat at such a pricey restaurant? The answer was never.

While she tucked in, she noticed Jared's attack on the sumptuous food was just as enthusiastic. She asked, and discovered he'd skipped lunch too. Watching him eat was as much a treat as watching him work. He gave both tasks the same enthusiasm and undivided attention and she knew with a quiet certainty that rippled through her feminine places that he'd give the same to a lover.

'Dessert?' Jared asked a while later when the main dishes had been cleared away and she'd more or less calmed down, for the moment at least.

'Yes, please.'

'Allow me to order for both of us.' He motioned the waiter.

'As long as it's loaded with calories.'

He smiled at her then referred to the menu, indicated his choice. 'For two, please.' A corner of his mouth tipped up. 'I guarantee you'll like it.'

A short time later, she stared at the plate the waiter had set between them. She felt the colour rising up her neck, bleeding into her cheeks, and thanked the little red tea light on their table for its camouflaging effect.

Italian blackberry Frangelico torte, she was informed. With a mountain of whipped cream.

Blackberries and cream…well, it was an obvious choice, wasn't it? Bolstered by a couple of glasses of bubbly, she met Jared's eyes across the table. Amusement flashed back at her.

In spite of herself, she couldn't help the wry little twist of her lips. 'And here's Pam telling me you don't have a sense of humour.'

He leaned back in his chair. 'Pam said that?'

She toyed with the stem of her wine glass and ventured, 'Maybe it's her way of saying you should loosen up some.'

He cocked his head as if the notion was absurd. 'And what do you think?'

'From what I've seen in the office today, she may have a point. Then again, there's this other side she obviously hasn't seen that kind of balances everything out.'

His lips curved. 'You're talking about my sharp wit and immeasurable charm.'

'Naturally.'

His smile widened to a grin for a split second, but then it faded and something other than humour stole into his eyes. Something darker, harder, more ruthless. He was silent a moment, staring into space. 'I run a multimillion-dollar company, Sophie. It's my life's ambition, my reason to get up in the morning, my passion.' He picked up his dessert spoon and drew circles on the heavy white cloth. 'Sometimes I forget that employees have priorities other than their nine-to-five job at Sanderson's.'

Sophie nodded. There was a sense of remoteness about him. As if he was used to distancing himself from the rest of the world. She picked her way carefully, watching his expression as she said, 'She also mentioned Crystal and Melissa and how you've been brilliant with them.'

His distance remained, his expression shut down. A barrier she couldn't cross. 'The business is the reason I've been able to afford to give my sisters something of what they've missed out on over the past twelve years. Enough about that. We've more interesting matters to discuss.'

His relaxed convivial demeanour returned as if he'd flicked a switch. How did he do that? she wondered. How could he turn his emotions off so easily and so completely? She only wished she had the same ability.

She finished the remainder of her wine while she studied the mouth-watering layers of hazelnut sponge, white chocolate and blackberry coulis in front of them.

'I ordered this concoction for a reason.'

'I can see that.' She was tempted to ask if he was going to feed it to her and watch her moan in pleasure. After all they both knew how the story went… She pressed her tingling lips together. Thank heavens they were in a public place because she was appalled to think how easily she'd let him seduce her if they were somewhere more private.

But as she watched him dip his spoon into the cake, add cream and lift it towards her mouth it was like falling into a hypnotic state.

Especially when he murmured, 'Open up, Sophie,' in that deep silky sexy timbre that made her think of dark chocolate… and a different set of circumstances when he might say those words.

He was thinking the same thing because his eyes seemed to take on a smoky gleam as he leaned closer, offering the spoon.

Her heart stopped, thumped once then pounded out a fast

rhythm and her mouth fell open of its own volition. He slid the cake between her lips. Smooth, slow, slippery. She couldn't look away—it was as if he held her captive. She sucked the delicious mouthful from the spoon. He'd engineered this sneaky… whatever-it-was…and she'd played right into his subversion.

'What's the verdict?' he asked.

'It's nice,' she managed. It wasn't only her tongue; every part of her was out of kilter. She gave herself a mental shake and made every attempt to pull herself together.

'*Nice?* Is that the best you can do?'

'Right now?' she snapped out—but quietly. 'Yes, it is.'

He grinned slowly. Using the same spoon, he scooped up another morsel and popped it into his own mouth. Still watching her. Still with that smoky gleam in his eyes.

She picked up her own spoon. 'Remember where we are.'

'And the reason we're here.'

She watched him through narrowed eyes while she ate. When she'd almost finished, she said, 'This dessert wasn't on the menu, was it? You ordered it specially.'

'It was worth it, don't you agree?'

'Your business dinner's a fake and we both know it.' She scooped up a final mouthful, then sat back and crossed her arms.

'No,' he said slowly, as if talking to a child. 'We do need to discuss Noosa.'

Suddenly it was decision time and she wasn't sure she knew the right answer. Or if he was even going to ask the question. 'I plan to spend the upcoming weekend familiarising myself wi—'

'I'm talking about after hours.' He cut her off with an impatient flick of his hand and his gaze pinned hers. 'And we both know it.'

Her words echoed back to her. At the same time, his eyes promised all manner of tempting after-hours delights and her insides flipped like a stack of pancakes. Beneath the table she twisted her hands together. 'Go ahead and talk.'

'Make no mistake, Noosa's been on the agenda a while.'

She nodded, knowing it was important to him that she understood he hadn't planned the whole thing to seduce her. 'Pam told me.'

'The way I see it, this is the perfect opportunity to explore this attraction we have. Get it out of our systems. Move on.'

Attraction. Physical, sexual. Mutual. She was still overawed with the knowledge that this dream of a guy was interested in her. For however long it took to 'move on'.

Was she game enough to go along with this? Experienced enough? To play it casual, have great sex—and it would be great sex with Jared Sanderson—then fly away to the other side of the world? She was leaving in three weeks and nothing and no one was going to stop her. So many ifs. Dream lovers were much less complicated.

But looking at the real man there *was* no comparison.

'If you're worried about repercussions,' he said, 'Pam'll probably be back at her desk by the time we return.' We can continue to see each other if we both decide that's what we still want.

'And your overseas plans won't be a problem,' he continued. 'We both know up front how it's going to be.'

Like a New Year sky-show, she thought. An explosion of sparks, heat and energy, over almost before it starts. And very terminal. Sky-shows also left an inevitable trail of cold ashy destruction as a reminder.

'So this…' she untangled her fingers, laid her palms flat on the table '…this…what we're going to "explore"…is a fling.'

He must have heard the doubt in her voice because he leaned across the table and covered the backs of her hands lightly with his—not soothing or reassuring so much as enticing. It sparkled all the way up her arms to her shoulders.

'You're not comfortable with that, are you?' he said. 'It's only a word, Sophie.'

'A word which conjures up other words like self-indulgence and irresponsibility.' *A good thing is only a good thing for as long as you enjoy it.*

He nodded slowly. 'So call it whatever you like.'

'A short term relationship,' she said. 'At least the word relationship implies a certain commitment, no matter how short-lived it may be. Don't worry,' she hurried on, 'I'm not looking for long term any more than you are.'

He looked at her kind of funny and she couldn't remember if he'd told her he wasn't looking for long term or whether she'd just assumed it. Of course he wasn't looking for more, she told herself, still holding his unreadable gaze. He didn't date the same woman for more than a few weeks.

She didn't date, period.

And yet, with Jared, even knowing all that, she felt…different somehow. Apart from being sexy he was a nice guy. Genuine. The kind of guy you could *maybe* trust. Maybe.

Turning her hands over so that his hard palms abraded her ultrasensitive ones, he laced his fingers through hers and his gaze seemed to reach down deep inside her to some unexplored place she'd never known existed. Maybe she was ready to take a chance on some fun with a guy. And since he'd enjoyed some fun at her expense, wouldn't it be kind of fun to tease this workaholic back just a little?

'So what do you say, are you with me?'

She just smiled a flirty smile and said, 'Tell you what, how about we have our coffee at my place?'

CHAPTER EIGHT

JARED leaned on Sophie's balcony and watched the palm fronds move lazily in the allotment across the street. A car-chase movie wailed from an open window in an apartment somewhere below. High-density living in apartments where the walls were thinner than cardboard wasn't for him. Then again, nowadays he could afford to be selective.

He knew Sophie's answer. Was one hundred and ten per cent certain. Didn't know why he'd asked the question. The question he was more interested in finding out the answer to right now was when did this short-term relationship start?

The brief drive back to her apartment had been…intense. Inside the car the tension had been so tight it had been almost explosive. Like sitting on a bunch of live wires.

Or maybe that had just been him.

She'd invited him into her cramped but cheerful living room with its hotchpotch mix of furniture and colour. Mostly maroon, cream and forest green with slashes of peach in the furnishings. She'd switched on a muted lamp then slid the balcony's full-length glass door open to catch the night breezes and invited him to make himself comfortable. He'd nearly laughed aloud at that and chosen the balcony, thankful for its cool camouflaging darkness.

She'd firmly refused his offer of help. Presumably, and some-what to his relief, she'd wanted to make the coffees herself.

He turned as she set two steaming aromatic mugs on her patio table in front of the open doorway. A muted gold light from the lamp spilled onto the balcony, leaving the far end with its potted palm draped in purple shadows.

'I'm afraid there's no such luxury as a cappuccino maker here. I…' She trailed off as she looked at him, and stood perfectly still.

Which gave him time to drink her in. Who needed coffee? She was glowing and beautiful and warmed his insides as no cappuccino could. She smelled of flowers in full bloom and hot velvet nights. Summer. No, he didn't want coffee. He'd waited all evening to reacquaint himself with her taste.

But before he could make his move she pulled the clasp from her hair and shook it free. An invitation if ever he saw one. He watched, transfixed, as the shiny black silk slithered loosely over her shoulders and down her back. The air between them smouldered with desire. With intent.

He wasn't aware that he'd crossed to her but here she was, an erratic pulse-beat away. In the half-light her skin was creamy smooth, her lips ripe and full, her eyes huge and aware. Then his fingers were skimming her jaw, angling her chin towards him. Up close he could pick out the subtle fragrance of sun-drenched petunias.

His heart seemed to stutter, his throat dried up. Right now he had no words to tell her how gorgeous she looked, how desirable. How much he wanted her. He lowered his mouth to hers.

Her body softened instantly against his, allowing him to pull her closer, to slide his hands beneath her hair and over her bare shoulders, down her spine to where the top of her dress fitted just below her shoulder blades.

She shifted with a moan that vibrated through his senses and settled in his throbbing groin. Her arms slid up and around his neck as she fitted herself against him. Her breasts rubbed against his chest. Her legs tangled with his. The smouldering heat threatened to spontaneously combust them both right where they stood.

And then, on the little table, his phone buzzed.

He almost lifted his head but suddenly something inside him rebelled. Years of putting everyone else first. Being there. Taking charge. He tightened his hold. Always-on-hand Jared was, at this moment—and for however many moments it might take—unavailable. With his fingers splayed against her back, he pressed her nearer, as if that might make the noise disappear.

But Sophie wasn't of the same mind. She drew back breathless, her hands still on his shoulders, and looked up at him. 'You want to get that?' she murmured.

'No.' No way. No. Not in a million years. 'It'll go to voicemail.'

The offensive sound ceased. He slid a finger along her collarbone, turned on just watching her lick her lips, wet from their kiss. 'Now…where were we…?' Putting her arms back in place around his neck, he nibbled at her mouth, *not* thinking about whether whoever-it-was had left a message and whether it might be important.

But, no matter how hard he tried, the moment was spoiled. He wanted to howl. Years of owning a business, and, more importantly, being there for his younger siblings, made it impossible to disregard the phone no matter how badly he wanted to make it with Sophie.

And he could already feel her cooling off. There was a tiny tremor of tension that hadn't been there before, as if she'd suddenly realised where this had been heading and come to her senses.

He only wished he felt as cool.

With a sigh he touched his forehead to hers. 'I'm going to have to see who that is first so I can ignore them guilt-free.'

She drew back. 'Timing,' she said, nodding as if she knew what she was talking about. 'Maybe it's a good thing it happened after all.'

'How can it be a good thing?' he muttered, stalking to the table. He swiped up the phone. One missed call from Lissa.

His pulse spiked in a different way when he remembered she'd gone out tonight. She'd left a message…

'Um, hi, Jared. Are you coming home any time soon? This is real dumb and I'm sorry and all, but I've locked myself out of Fort Knox. Any chance you can swing by and let me in?'

He closed his eyes and prayed for patience and understanding. Because right now he didn't have much of either.

'Is everything okay?' Sophie's soft voice reminding him of what might have been.

He opened his eyes but he turned away, didn't look at her. 'Melissa's managed to lock herself out,' he clipped, already returning her call.

Melissa answered on the first ring. 'Jared. Good, you got my message. Um…did I disturb you?'

He unclenched his teeth before they cracked. 'Why didn't your friends wait with you?' And why so early? She didn't usually stroll home till three. He fisted his free hand against his trousers and tried to maintain an outwardly calm and composed façade.

'I've got a headache so I caught a cab home and it was gone before I realised I'd forgotten my keys,' she said. 'I didn't notice because I left first and wasn't the one who locked the door tonight—you were. Sorry, are you…busy? I can—'

'Stay right there. I'll be home in ten minutes.' He swung around to Sophie. He wasn't going to make it with her tonight. 'Lissa's not feeling well, I have to go.'

'Yeah, you do.'

'I'm sorry about the coffee. I'll ring you.' He paused on his way to the front door to look back at her. She was still watching him with that wide expressive and slightly stunned gaze. 'What are you doing this weekend?' He realised he'd never asked his PA that question in quite that tone nor with the same interest and expectation.

The rush of surprised excitement in her eyes was quickly doused. 'I'm going to keep Pam company since she can't go out in public. I've got chick flicks, calamine lotion, chocolate ripple ice cream and a book of cryptic crosswords.'

He had to grin at the cosy scenario. 'Sounds like you've got all bases covered there.' So Sophie was the kind of person who was willing to put her weekend on hold for a friend. She knew what he was offering but she'd turned him down because she was needed elsewhere. Putting her needs aside. *Not so selfish as you profess, are you, Sophie Buchanan?*

He understood all too well. He also knew she understood why he had to leave now. He opened the front door, stepped onto the common balcony. 'I'll be in Brisbane first thing Monday morning and back late Tuesday.'

Sophie caught up with him, curled her hand around the door. 'Have a successful trip.'

He nodded briefly. 'Any problems, ring me.' His tone sounded brusque to his own ears as he turned abruptly away. Abrupt because he had to force himself not to touch her again. Because if he kissed her goodnight, he'd not want to stop at one and Liss was waiting and it was well past midnight.

Sophie was glad to have something to do over the weekend. During the day, Pam's companionship took her focus away from Jared. It was a different story at night when she lay on hot sheets and her body itched and burned so that she had to wonder if she was coming down with chicken pox too.

She watched the stars track across the night sky. She knew she and Jared would have ended up in bed if he hadn't been called away. Overwhelmed by the burning tension between them on her balcony and his obvious intention to take things further, she'd let her hair down. Literally.

She'd never played the seductress role but with Jared... well...it was different... And there'd been just enough wine in her system to loosen her up and free that inner woman she'd denied for so long.

Maybe he was the best thing to ever happen to her.

No. She shook her head against her pillow. She couldn't allow herself to think that. *Would not.* She had to keep her focus on her future. *Hers.* She was going overseas. Her goal, her life. He was just that fling she'd fantasised about.

'Yes, *fling*,' she declared into the darkness. And, as she'd stated to him on her opinion of flings, it was going to be self-indulgent and irresponsible. *And risky,* a little voice whispered.

But didn't she deserve one self-absorbed, giddy and reckless performance before she turned thirty? Only two years away.

She pushed away the melancholy thought that by that age she'd always expected to be happily married with her boisterous brood of three kids and assorted pets.

Circumstances changed, expectations changed accordingly.

Back at the office on Monday morning there was a mountain of work and preparation to be done before Wednesday. She shook her head when she reread the report she'd written, jabbed the delete key and started over. It seemed that every two minutes Jared popped into her mind. His name, the way he kissed, something he'd said, making her flustered and forgetful and somehow rendering her incapable of stringing together a coherent sentence, let alone transferring it to the computer.

What was this? There didn't seem to be any room in her mind for anything else but him. Nothing like it had ever happened to her before. Not with Glen, and he'd been the only man she'd dated seriously and she'd married him at eighteen.

Jared phoned on Tuesday afternoon to make final arrangements for their trip. Because she hadn't been expecting to hear his voice, her heart did a stop-start and her pulse *rat-a-tat-tatted*. He made her feel like a ditsy teenager, self-conscious and giggly.

She couldn't wait to see him again. Since when had she felt that way? It was dangerously like missing someone. Nowadays she made sure her happiness didn't depend on other people. So how was it possible? And she'd only known him a few days.

And then it was Wednesday.

Jared was picking her up soon after lunch, which gave Sophie time to ransack her bag and cull unnecessaries. To add an extra jacket. At the last minute she fretted over today's choice of attire. Casual or business? She eventually decided on something comfortable yet feminine. She was changing her monotone white trousers and blouse for a more vibrant silky knit dress when he knocked.

Her heart jumped into her mouth at the commanding sound. He was early again. She'd wanted to be super relaxed and in control when he arrived and she was anything but.

She sucked in a deep calming breath before opening the door. 'Hi.' Her voice still came out more breathless than she would have liked.

'Hi, yourself.'

His eyes met hers and seemed to brighten to the colour of moss. She raised a hand to the door jamb. There really was something about that creased cheek that made her weak at the knees and tipped her off-centre. Which was why her gaze took a quick southern slide...

And *ooh, yeah*...what Jared did for a pair of jeans. Dark denim faded in all the right places and tight where it counted.

She dragged her gaze up—and over a blinding white Ralph Lauren polo shirt with Sanderson's logo screen-printed in navy over one solid-looking pectoral. Top two buttons undone, a few wisps of dark masculine hair, prominent Adam's apple, a tiny C-shaped scar where maybe he'd nicked himself shaving once upon a time...

'Nice dress,' he said, and she realised while she'd been eyeing him up he'd been returning the favour. 'Orange suits you.'

'Orange.' She screwed up her nose and clucked her tongue—

such a common and inadequate word for such a beautiful colour. 'Stormy sunrise.'

'Even better.' He grinned. Another blinding moment. Then his grin sobered a bit and his eyes took on a sexy silvery glint as he reached for her rolling suitcase at her side. 'Maybe we'll see one of those together in the next couple of days.'

'Oh?' she replied, casually ignoring his meaning as she locked her door. 'Did they forecast bad weather?'

'Blue skies all the way.' He smiled, then headed for the elevator.

She followed him inside the lift without comment. Ridiculous not to now when they'd already shared more than just air and were about to get even closer in the next couple of days.

A moment later she settled into his luxury convertible for the three-hour drive. It was, as Jared had promised, blue skies, and a lovely day to be on the road rather than stuck inside an office somewhere.

Before they turned onto the Pacific Motorway, which would take them past Brisbane and on to the Sunshine Coast, Jared asked, 'Do you mind if we call in at Crystal's place on the way?'

The question seemed to come out of the blue and jolted Sophie right out of her comfort zone. 'No, of course not. Is she okay?'

'Fine. She came home from hospital on Saturday and Ian took a few days off, but it's her first day on her own with the bub and Ian's working late tonight to catch up. She asked if I'd drop by.'

'If you ask me, I think Jared just wants another look at his niece.' Sophie smiled his way and saw his mouth kick up at the edge.

They pulled up outside a cream brick home surrounded by several palms and a high fence. 'I'll just wait here…' She didn't want to intrude, nor did she want to see a newborn baby and experience the associated emotions that went with it.

He turned in his seat to face her. A puzzled frown puckered his brow. 'Crystal's expecting to meet you. I told her we couldn't stay long.'

'You told her about me?'

'I told her my temporary PA was accompanying me to Noosa, yeah.'

Oh. Of course. A tinge of embarrassment stung her cheeks and she smiled casually to cover it, glad she was wearing her sunglasses. 'This is a family time…I mean there's a million things she'll be catching up on—sleep, or feeding…'

'She's not. I spoke to her just before I picked you up.' He tossed his sunglasses on the dash and swung open his door. 'Come on, five minutes.'

Sophie followed. What else could she do? She didn't want to see the baby, or, worse, to be asked if she wanted a hold. And she just knew neither of them would understand. They would think her rude. Still, she could be lucky. New babies slept a lot. Didn't they? Sometimes.

Tension snapped her spine straight all the way to the door, where they were greeted by a gorgeous golden retriever who raced around from the side of the house.

'Meet Goldie.' Jared ruffled the dog's fur. 'Hello, girl.' Her eyes drooled adoration up at him as he caught the expressive face in his hands, and was rewarded with a sloppy kiss.

'Oh, isn't she beautiful?' Sophie crouched beside Jared to join in the petting. 'Do you have pets?'

'No. Our much-loved and ancient Betsy died a few years back. I'm too busy to train a new puppy and now that Lissa's home less and less,…it wouldn't be fair on the dog.'

But Sophie saw the fleeting shadow that crossed his gaze before his sister opened the door.

'Great meeting you, Sophie.' A remarkably hassle-free-looking Crystal led the way to her kitchen. 'I've heard a lot about you.'

Sophie looked to Jared, who shrugged his shoulders and

blamed Lissa. He set the bag of supplies on a table crammed at one end with baby products and a florist's arrangement of pink blooms that were starting to wilt, then promptly disappeared down a hallway, presumably to see his niece.

Unlike Melissa, who shared no apparent familial traits with Jared, Crystal was the feminine epitome of her brother. Same tall, dark, green-eyed attractiveness. And looking amazing considering she'd given birth only a week ago.

They chatted a few moments while Crystal unloaded an unlikely selection of disposable nappies, pâté and crackers and a fresh pineapple from Jared's eco-bag. She was as easy-going as Melissa. Both sisters obviously thought the world of Jared and seemed to be ever-so-subtly interested in Sophie's life.

Sophie was starting to relax and think that it was about time they got moving when Crystal said, 'You have to meet Arabella before you go.'

Oh. Sophie bit the inside of her lip. 'I wouldn't want to disturb...'

But Crystal was already leading the way and the last thing Sophie wanted to do was offend the new mother in any way, shape or form. These days she was experienced at masking her feelings. No one would know that inside where it was just her, her heart was still crying over her once-in-a-million miracle that had never had a chance.

Sophie could smell the baby's room from the end of the hall. It streamed through her senses. The lovely soft scent of powder and silky skin and newness. Crystal showed her into the room and Sophie made a valiant attempt to lose the melancholy.

Jared was leaning over the bassinet, stroking the infant's cheek. And *he* was the one making goo-goo noises. He turned when they entered, his expression full of pride and pleasure. 'She's just waking up.' He looked to his sister. 'May I?'

Crystal set a pile of baby clothes on the blanket box. 'Go right ahead. Just remember the clean nappy by your left arm's included in part of the picking-up ritual.'

'Fine by me.'

Somewhere a phone rang. 'I'll just get that,' she said and left the room.

Sophie watched Jared pick his niece up with infinite tenderness and care, cradling her fuzzy-topped head in his palm. The rest of her fitted snug along the length of his forearm.

'There you are, princess.' There was a smile and love in his voice as he tucked her closer. 'Uncle Jared's got you, you lucky girl, you.' Princess chewed on her fist while unfocused eyes of an indefinable colour stared up at him.

Sophie had never seen anything more beautiful or more powerful than the sight of this tiny fragile infant against Jared's tanned, hard and muscular arms. It was one of those life-affirming moments and the pity of it was that she didn't think uncle noticed.

Made for fatherhood. The fleeting thought skimmed the edge of her consciousness. She'd heard people talking about a woman being made to be a mother but had never applied the parenthood tag to a male. But yes, she thought, watching the muscles in his arms twist and bunch as he adjusted his hold, that was what he was. His arms were as capable of holding babies as they'd be accomplished at holding a woman.

Her heart swelled and blossomed and seemed to open up like the petals of a flower.

Because right here, right now, she was falling for him.

It wasn't his looks or wealth or charm, they were just side benefits. No, it was much more basic and simple than that. It was his underlying goodness, his empathy for others, his honesty. Core values she shared.

One day he'd make some woman very happy. His wife, the mother of his children would never want for anything. But it wouldn't be Sophie. It *couldn't* be Sophie.

His eyes looked unexpectedly her way, catching her watching him. Catching her thoughts? She hoped not, and drew herself up, eyeballing him boldly, daring him to take issue with them.

But he only said, 'Want a hold?'

At first she was afraid her voice wouldn't work, but luckily her 'not today,' didn't carry the emotion she held inside. She forced a laugh to cover the wretched awkwardness. 'I'd probably drop her or something.'

'No, you wouldn't.' He stared at her a moment, eyes slightly narrowed. She could see the questions shuffling behind his eyes.

'Babies and I don't hit it off.' She shrugged carelessly. 'They take one look at me and it's waterworks.'

'Not with Arabella, she's too young yet.' He kissed her nose. 'Aren't you, sweetheart?' But to Sophie's relief he didn't pursue her protest, preferring to talk some more *ga-ga* to his niece. He lowered the infant onto the change table and managed the nappy-change process with the same skill and confidence he used to conduct a business meeting.

And, oh... Rather than detract from Jared's powerful masculinity, the child he tended simply added another dimension to the already multifaceted man she was coming to know. Her legs almost sagged beneath her and something rolled over in her chest. She was, without a doubt, looking at a picture-perfect poster for the sexiest man alive.

She turned away.

She needed to remember a couple of important things. One. Jared wasn't a one-woman man. Second, she was leaving Australia. And top of the list, she reminded herself a man who loved kids this much could never be the man for her.

No man could.

CHAPTER NINE

SINCE Sophie had never travelled up this way and seemed so enraptured with the passing scenery, Jared let her indulge in relative silence, pointing out places of interest on the way.

One thing was certain, she wasn't looking for home and family. He'd seen the almost panicked look in her eyes when he'd asked her if she wanted to hold Arabella. He drummed his fingers lightly on the steering wheel as Brisbane's hazy skyline came into view in the distance.

She was the most skittish woman around babies he'd ever seen. She'd shown zero interest in the baby shop in Coolangatta. Too much so, in fact. Had only met Arabella because basic courtesy required it. She'd admitted she had no interest in tying herself down with kids.

Like someone else he'd known. Bianca had kept her no-kids policy to herself until she'd discovered Jared intended Melissa to be a part of their lives after they married. Bianca might have reconsidered his proposal but he knew it would never have worked in the long run. He'd counted himself lucky he'd found out before he'd made a commitment. No second chances.

At least with Sophie he knew everything up front. Short term was all they were looking for. When it happened, his children would be wanted and loved by both parents. But settling down was years into the future. The years he should have been out drinking till dawn and getting laid had been spent being a responsible guardian to his sisters, and he had some catching up to do.

He was looking forward to doing some of that catching up with Sophie these next couple of days.

'Spectacular, don't you agree?'

Jared's voice somewhere behind her, plush velvet stroking over her shoulders and down her back.

'Very.' Sophie stood in the middle of the room, not knowing where to look first. This palatial riverfront home was *their* home for the next couple of days. And nights.

It was the ever-present thoughts about those nights that had her nerves twitching and her hormones bouncing like lottery balls on a Saturday night. She quashed them quickly, focusing on the here and now. It was more than spectacular, it was over-the-top dazzling.

White-tiled flooring and furniture flowed outwards in all directions, giving the impression it went on for ever. A few touches of blue and lime green in the cushions or decorative art invoked a cool sense of peace and tranquillity. Extending out from the patio was a private jetty where one could moor their luxury yacht, and on the other side of the river in the reddening haze of sunset she could see other multimillion-dollar homes.

Turn to the right and she could see the master bedroom and its snowy white king-size bed reflected in the turquoise infinity pool off the main living area. Floor-to-ceiling sliding glass doors in both rooms virtually allowed one to swim to the bedroom if one so desired.

Of course they'd taken separate bedrooms. One had to act the part of a PA to begin with at least and she still needed some privacy at this point in their relationship.

Right now her thoughts were on the upcoming business dinner in a little over an hour and she needed to turn herself into the professional Jared expected. She didn't have time for the heat she saw in his eyes that promised to make them late.

'I'm…ah…going to jump in the shower.'

His eyes darkened. 'Do you need your back scrubbed?'

Her blood warmed, her skin tingled. He hadn't moved a muscle but Sophie had the impression he'd come closer. She had no doubt he was well skilled in scrubbing backs, making fast, furious love and getting to his meetings on time.

Not her... At least she didn't *think* so. 'Do you want this new client on your books?' she said, turning away before she decided to test the theory for herself. She headed for the refuge of her en-suite bathroom.

She felt the smile in his voice when, from behind her, he said, 'If you change your mind just give a yell.'

Her lips curved. 'If you hear me yell you have my full permission to come right on in and to hell with being professionally punctual,' she tossed over her shoulder as she walked away.

As refuges went it was a marble palace—all white with gold fittings, fernery spilling from hanging pots and warm downlights that turned her paler-than-average skin colour—especially the parts not normally exposed—a flattering honey tone. She twisted her hair up and clasped it on top of her head.

Setting the water to moderately hot, she stepped beneath the spray. Under the circumstances she really didn't need hot, but when it came to her shower she was a creature of habit...

A squelchy squirming sensation beneath her toes had her jumping back and glancing down. She saw a centipede—longer and thicker than her middle finger—its hideous body writhing in the shower stall at her feet. *And they bite...*

But it was the way it thrashed about that had the blood-curdling scream springing from her lips while her fingers scrabbled for the shower-screen door. *Get out! Get out!*

'What's wrong?' Loud knocking on the door. 'Sophie?'

'Get it out!' Through the glass enclosure, she was aware of Jared bursting into the room but her eyes were pinned to the sight inches from her toes while she struggled to open the door. She finally got the door to slide and all but fell out of the

shower, backing up as far away as she could. 'That...*that*...' It was all she could get past her constricted throat.

Shutting the water off, Jared reached for the wooden handled back scrub hanging beneath the shower head and she screwed her eyes shut...

Water trickled down her cooling body as she clasped her arms around her and heard a series of loud knocks. A convulsive shiver shuddered down her spine. 'Oh, *God*.' She didn't want to know how he'd done it, only that he had. 'Is it dead? Is it gone?'

'It's dead.' She heard the toilet flush. 'And now it's gone.'

A tortured sigh escaped her lips. Only then did she take it all in. She was naked. He wore jeans, nothing else. She slid her eyes to his, willing him to do the same.

To his gentlemanly credit, his gaze remained locked with hers. Not even a flicker of a glance where it shouldn't go. He reached for a towel on the rail beside him, passed it to her.

'Thanks.' She grabbed it and pulled it in front of herself. Shivering. With cold or relief or excitement? 'Just so you know, I'm not one of those squealy women,' she felt compelled to point out. 'Normally. But those...' She shuddered again.

'Okay.' He didn't move a muscle. But there was a flicker of movement at one corner of his mouth saying maybe he believed her, maybe not.

'I'm going to get back in there now,' she said, as much to herself as to him. Then another flesh-crawling thought... 'You don't think it came up the drain, do you? What if it has a mate somewhere...'

'I don't know. Maybe you should let me stay here and make sure.' There was a roguish light in those eyes, a hint of the devil in his chivalrous words. He reached into the stall and switched the water back on for her.

Then—and she didn't know what demon possessed her... yes she did and his name was Jared Sanderson—she tossed the towel on the floor and stepped under the water. 'Maybe I should.' Her heart was hammering, her blood coursing hotly through her veins. *Take a chance, be that sensual woman you want to be.* Knowing she was starting something she might not be able to stop, keeping her back to him, she dangled her soap-filled sponge-on-a-string over one shoulder. 'And maybe I should let you be useful and wash my back while you wait.'

She felt him take the sponge and, oh, that first glide across her shoulders was warm, slow and reassuringly impersonal. Another pass, this time down her spine, stopping at her waist. Then pressure at the base of her neck.

She inhaled sharply. 'That's not my sponge…'

'No.'

Thumbs. Working tensed muscles in her neck. Then hands. Slick, soapy hands that began at her nape and slid across her shoulders. Down either side of her spine and over the curve of her waist, fingers both tantalisingly close to the sides of her breasts and frustratingly far away.

And she maybe shouldn't have let him start… Her breathing grew heavy. So did her breasts—heavy and tight and full. She wanted to turn around and let him give them the same slow, slick attention.

His hands slid lower and cupped her bottom. Her feminine core grew hot, her breaths quickened. But when his thumbs dipped between her butt cheeks, then lightly down the backs of her thighs, her legs sagged and she braced her hands on the tiles in front of her for support. *'Jared.'*

'Right here, honey,' he murmured, his lips so close she could feel his breath hot on her ear. He'd stepped into the shower— she could smell the wet denim—but the only part of him in contact with her were his hands.

And what contact.

'This was a bad idea…' She gasped when his exploration grew bolder, his fingers delved deeper. Too deep. Not nearly deep enough…

'You don't really think that,' he assured her.

'Oh. Yes. I. Do.' She was so breathless she couldn't seem to get out more than one word at a time between shallow gulps of air.

'So you want me to stop…' His hands moved away.

'Yes. *No*,' she moaned.

She heard his soft chuckle, then sent up a prayer of thanks when his newly soaped-up hands skimmed her waist and came around to cup her breasts. Holding their weight in his palms, he massaged and teased, swirling his fingertips around her tight nipples and sending sensation spiralling to her core and lower, between her thighs.

Steam billowed and swirled around them like an intimate cloak. Just the two of them in their own private steam bath. The water pelting her now oversensitised body felt like hot hailstones and sounded harsh in the stall's confines.

She squirmed as the ache between her legs intensified. Moving her legs farther apart, she arched her back and begged him silently to, 'Touch me.'

She hadn't realised she'd spoken aloud but her whispered plea sounded harsh and desperate in the humid air and not like her at all. And then one of his hands was between her thighs, fingernails cruising along her slippery cleft, the fingers of his other hand rolling a nipple, teasing it into almost unbearable hardness.

'Like this?' he whispered against her ear and plunged his fingers inside her. He withdrew them slowly, drawing out the wetness along her sensitised flesh and making her moan some more.

Her legs trembled like stalks of wheat in a rain storm. She leaned her forehead against the cool tiles as well as her hands. 'Yes.' *Exactly like that.*

He repeated his exquisite torture. And again. Over and over, each thrust of his fingers more erotic, more persuasive. His lips nuzzled her neck then bit gently, possessively, and his voice was thick with arousal when he said, 'You're so hot. So deliciously wet.'

His explicit words, the skilful way he touched her, as if he'd known her body for years, the sound of his voice against her ear sent her soaring up, up, up. Over the silky precipice on a low heartfelt cry, her body convulsing around his fingers.

'Oh. *Wow*,' she whispered when she'd got her breath back. His hands trailed over her thighs, then away.

But when she finally turned, she saw nothing but steam and a trail of water across the tiles. He was gone.

Like a dream.

How did you walk into a room to face *your boss* as if you hadn't just been given the most intense orgasm of your life? Sophie wondered as she stared at her reflection in the bedroom mirror. She adjusted the collar on the cream dress and asked herself how did you face that boss, the one who'd given you that orgasm, over a business dinner as if your private parts weren't still on fire and already aching for more?

Grabbing her jacket and purse from the chair, she headed for the living room. She was about to find out.

He was wearing a charcoal suit and baby-blue pinstriped shirt with matching blue tie and watching the local news on the ginormous flat-screen TV on the wall. His short hair was still damp and his fresh foresty scent drifted in the warm air.

His gaze flicked to hers across the expanse of tiled floor. Dark, hungry, slightly desperate. As if he wanted to eat her alive and wanted nothing to do with her at the same time. And she could hardly blame him. As earth-shattering as her climax had been, it hadn't exactly been a mutually shared and satisfying experience.

'Hi,' she said, since he didn't seem inclined to speak.

He looked her up and down, then his eyes lingered on her bare legs and she saw his jaw clench.

'Is it too short? It's too short.' She should have gone for the mid-calf green instead of the above-the-knee. Thoughtless under the circumstances. 'I'll ch—'

'It's not too short.' He cleared the huskiness from his throat and a little of the tension eased from his features. 'It's fine just the way it is. You look lovely.'

'Thanks. So do you. Well, not *lovely* exactly,' she babbled on. 'More smart, savvy businessman.'

'I'm not sure how smart and savvy this businessman's going to be this evening.' Flicking off the TV with the remote, he crossed to her, curled hard fingers around her upper arms. 'I didn't play it too damn smart back there in the bathroom.' His olive-green eyes turned to unreadable slate and he dropped his hold as if he'd been stung.

Her cheeks burned, sparks shot through her bloodstream. Her body was already clamouring for an encore of his sexpertise and *he regretted it*?

Jared clamped his jaw shut. She looked like a fantasy in that nude-coloured dress and black shoes. And if he stood here a microsecond longer looking into those molten amber eyes and knowing he was responsible for putting the heat in them, he'd lose his tenuous hold on control and his *smart savvy business* reputation really would be a memory. Turning away, he strode to the door. 'Let's go.'

The deal was in the bag. Jared already knew. The groundwork had been done over the past month and tonight was more of a social event.

Sophie was the perfect PA and partner. She involved Trent's wife Tania in girl talk, leaving him free to discuss plans and possibilities with Trent, but was eerily able to switch to business when he needed her to. She'd obviously swotted up on the information over the weekend because she was conversant and up-to-date with the project.

It had been a terminally long dinner, but Trent was meeting

them tomorrow to show them over the property and sign off on the deal.

But then their hosts wanted to show them a little local hospitality and it was on to the newest supper club to listen to the latest jazz/blues trio over a cheese and wine nightcap.

It was torture sitting so close to Sophie that he could smell the soap she'd used—the soap he'd used, actually—and not being able to touch her the way he wanted to. Not as a boss but as something more. For the short time they had before she left he wanted to know Sophie better. A lot better.

A couple of times their thighs had bumped beneath the table and their eyes connected—a brief clash of heat—before she shifted position and resumed conversation. With Tania, with Trent. Not him. Since this was business, *his* business, there was nothing he could do about it now, and she knew it. She was driving him mad. Payback, no doubt, for the way he'd left the situation hanging on their way out this evening when he'd dropped her arms as if she had some terminal infectious disease.

He had a few ideas for payback himself.

It was nearly midnight before they said their goodnights to the clients. The journey back to their accommodation took less than five minutes. During that time Sophie went into PA mode with tomorrow's plans. A meeting at ten to discuss a new project, a couple of client follow-ups, signing the deal with Trent…

He knew it backwards; he'd given her the instructions for the damn schedule in the first place.

He pressed the remote and the security door rolled up, rolled down as he drove through and parked undercover at the side of the house. He killed the engine. Unclicked his seat belt with unnecessary force. 'That's enough.' She stopped speaking immediately. 'Your PA duties are over for the evening.'

'Okay.' She chewed on her lip a moment, then turned to face him, disengaged her own seat belt.

He couldn't read her eyes in the dimness. 'Sophie. Honey.' He caressed the side of her face. Noticed his fingers all but trembled. 'You misunderstood me earlier when I said what happened in the bathroom wasn't a smart move.'

She tilted her head to one side, as if to say 'go on'.

He caught her face between his hands. 'If I'd touched you again I'd've had you on the floor with that dress up around your ears before you could blink and we'd never have made it to dinner.'

She gave a tiny gasp and her fingers worked at the neckline of her dress.

He shook his head. 'If that sounded crude, I apologise. You've been driving me to distraction all evening. All week. I'm going crazy. Do you know how hard it's been all evening? Watching you and not being able to touch you?'

'No. I can't begin to imagine…' a corner of her mouth kicked up, a smile that spread to her cheeks and twinkled into her eyes as she looked pointedly down at his swollen crotch '…how hard. But if you take me indoors maybe you can show me.'

He sat back and watched her gaze heat as she reached for his tie, slid it through her fingers. 'And for the record I'd really, really like for you to have me on the floor. Dress around my ears and all. It's a personal fantasy of mine.'

'Be sure you know what you're asking.' His voice came out rough-edged, harsh in the car's close confines as he ripped off his tie.

She shook her head. 'I know exactly what.'

CHAPTER TEN

A QUIVER of excitement thrummed through Sophie as Jared gripped her upper arms and pulled her against him. His mouth crashed down on hers, demanding. His fingers plucked at her nipples through her dress, arousing. His breath was harsh and fast and hot against her cheek and she shivered in anticipation.

This wasn't the charming, focused entrepreneur she'd spent the evening with. Nor was he the suave and skilled and generous lover who'd sent her into ecstasy in the shower earlier. That man had been a man in control.

This man was not and the knowledge that Sophie was the woman to bring out this wild, desperate side sang through her body like fine wine. Feminine power. She'd never experienced it, and it felt amazing. Her blood frizzled beneath her skin wherever he took those impatient hands and clever mouth.

Quick as a snap he had the zip in her dress shirring down her back. His mouth was hot and wet on her neck as he slipped the dress off her shoulders. 'I want you…'

'Yes…' she breathed, quivering at the edge of desperation she heard in his voice.

Quick deft fingers plunged beneath the edge of her bra to tweak her already hard nipples into throbbing points of lust. He yanked the bra cups down. 'I want you *now*.' His urgency sent hot shivers down her spine.

Closing her eyes, she arched her aching breasts upwards. 'Yes. Right now.'

And she would have let him take her right then, right there in the car with the squeak and smell of leather, the gearstick between them like some secondary phallus, but he was out of the car, opening her door, pulling her out.

He tugged her to the front of the car, somehow losing her dress on the way, and splayed her across the slippery smooth bonnet to feast on her semi-exposed breasts like some primeval starving animal.

The heat of the car's engine warmed her back and buttocks, cool damp air caressed her décolletage. A hard thigh nudged her legs apart, one hand shot between them and up to find the edge of her panties.

And, oh, that first flick of his fingers over damp cotton… She sucked in a gasp as the small but electric sensation bolted to her core.

'Sophie…' It was a growl, as strong and dangerous as any predator, and she trembled, not with fear but with desire. Excitement. Anticipation.

One tug and his fingers twisted beneath her panties. He stroked her once, twice, then plunged inside. Her inner muscles quivered and clenched around his fingers.

Their gazes clashed. She stared in wonder, in awe. All trace of civilised gone, just primal aroused male. She could see it smoulder behind his night-darkened eyes, could feel it in the heat coming off his body in waves, could smell the musky scent of arousal on his skin.

And the long, hard and demanding ridge of masculinity against her thigh.

She wanted it inside her. She wanted him stretching her, invading her, filling her. *Ful*filling her. Yanking the annoying clasp from her hair, she shook her hair free, aware of the feminine nature of her action and revelling in it. 'Yes…*now*,' she ordered, leaning back on her elbows, spreading her legs wider for him and rocking against his hand.

With a sharp, ripping sound her panties were gone, tossed

away, leaving her fully exposed to Jared's hot eyes. There was a stunned moment of stillness from both of them. Then the want, the impatience.

'*Now, now, now.*' The fevered chant beat through her blood, keeping time with her frantic pulse.

Jared's fingers were so unsteady he could barely unzip his trousers. She didn't want finesse, neither did he. He could have given her words—how alluring she looked in starlight with her hair tumbled over her shoulders, her eyes hot for him, her dusky nipples glistening from his mouth, but she didn't want romantic words, neither did he.

Now, now, now.

The flames in his gut leapt higher at the husky sound of her ragged demand on the still evening air. She didn't want slow, neither did he.

Sliding his hands beneath her arms, he reached behind her back, flicked the catch on her bra. She pulled it off and sent it sailing behind her with an abandon that surprised him almost as much as it seemed to surprise her. She might have tossed her stilettos the same way but he shook his head. 'The shoes stay.'

He freed himself from his boxers while he muttered, 'Protection.'

She stared into his eyes for a beat longer than he expected before she said, 'Got it covered.'

Praise be to heaven for that.

No more waiting, no time to think. He plunged into her hot slippery sex in one swift glide. He knew it was only physical but the groan that erupted seemed to come from the very depths of his being.

Clamping her legs around his waist, she answered with a low keening sound of her own and latched onto his shoulders, her fingernails digging hard into his flesh. He relished the exquisite pain, returning the favour with lips and tongue and teeth on the delicate fragrant skin beneath her jaw.

She was the sweet new temptation of a spring morning, the sultry seductress of summer's heat. And wherever he led, she kept pace with him. To places of hot, dark pleasures and whirling dervishes and erotic delights.

He told himself it was all need and greed and speed yet... for an infinitesimal hiatus, there was a lifetime in her eyes. But there was no time to puzzle it, less to wonder. He drove faster, harder, until he heard her cry out as she came, the wonder of it as he lost himself inside her.

For a long moment he rested his head on her breast, listening to her heart's rapid pounding, his own heart beating in his ears while they both came down to earth. What had just happened here? Was this intensity normal? Surely it hadn't been so long he'd forgotten what it was like?

'You okay?' he murmured, moving his lips over her skin. He looked into her eyes.

She blinked at him. 'Mm-mm.' It was a lazy, satisfied sound. 'I reckon so.'

'I think I can just about feel my legs again. What say we find somewhere a little more comfortable?' Without waiting for an answer he carried her across the patio and inside.

He set her on her feet in front of the white leather couch and stared at her. With only the underwater lights from the pool beyond the window to lend them light, awe and...something more...filled him.

She was a picture of perfection. Her lips were ripe, full, thoroughly kissed, her eyes wide and soulful, her long bare legs, dainty feet crammed in the sexiest pair of shoes he'd ever seen. Who was this dishevelled Sophie with her hair a tangled dark halo, her nipples pinched in the cool air? 'Are you cold?'

Sophie looked into his eyes and wondered who this woman was that she'd suddenly become. And how could she be cold bathed in all that stunning heat? She shook her head. 'But there is a problem here.'

He frowned. 'What?'

'I'm the only one naked. Hardly seems fair.'

A slow smile touched his lips. 'You're probably right.'

Her gaze drifted down his dishevelled torso. His shirt was crushed, his trousers hung open and low on his hips. She reached for his top shirt button. 'My turn, I think.'

She worked the rest of his buttons, then she was dragging the shirt aside so she could see if her dream lived up to the reality. To splay her hands over hard, bronzed skin sprinkled with dark hair. 'So hot,' she murmured, then leaned forward to press a kiss over his heart and feel the strong beat beneath her lips.

Still stroking his skin with its hard muscle beneath, she flicked her tongue around a tight male nipple. A tingle of salt, a whiff of masculine soap, the unique scent that was Jared. Sliding her hands over his shoulders, she eased the shirt off his arms. The immediate urgency over for the next few moments at least, she continued her journey of exploration in a leisurely, indulgent fashion.

Enjoying her newly discovered feminine power, she tugged the waistband lower and ordered, 'Everything off. Now.'

'Bossy little creature, aren't you?' he murmured, voice tinged with amusement.

When he'd obliged, she took a moment to admire the view. Gorgeous. Perfect. She had to touch. So many places. So many textures. He reigned over Michelangelo's David any day... *Venice, Rome.*

Her joy in the moment slipped a little. Soon she'd be far from here and this would be a memory. And it could never be anything more with him. This afternoon with baby Arabella had confirmed she'd never be the woman for Jared.

Oh, but what if she could? Rather than meet his gaze, she pressed her lips to his chest. What if he didn't care that she couldn't have kids? What if he could love her for who she was and it would be enough?

Love? She yanked herself back. Whatever was she thinking?

'Regrets?'

'Oh, no.' Now she met his eyes. 'No. I was thinking, that's all.'

'Sad thoughts.' He slid his arms around her and held her close. And his skin when it touched hers was like fire, intensely arousing yet quietly comforting at the same time.

'I've seen that look in your eyes already today,' he murmured, his words muffled against her hair.

'No.' She had to be more careful. Keep her guard up around him. She mustn't let him see. It was all about good times for the next couple of weeks. She wouldn't let herself think beyond that. 'You imagine too much.'

And she kissed his chin and smiled into those perceptive eyes. Her fingers busied themselves lower down and she saw his gaze change from concern to arousal and felt him stir to life again in her hands. She blinked and ran a thumb over the silky tip. 'Already?'

He grinned. 'Just give me a few minutes.'

She wondered how long it had been since he'd been with a woman.

She let him tug her down onto the wide leather couch. They lay close in companionable silence for a moment, staring up at the underwater light from the pool reflecting on the ceiling. Somewhere across the water drifted the distant sound of wind chimes.

'Tell me about him.'

She frowned in the darkness. Just when she thought he'd forgotten about it… 'Who?'

'The guy from your home town. The reason you left.'

'How do you…?' She trailed off. That first day on the way to Coolangatta she'd talked about a 'change of scenery' and avoided mentioning him because it was none of Jared's business. But Jared was the kind of guy who made you want to share. 'That would be my ex-husband.'

She felt him shift, felt his gaze on her. 'You were married?'

She kept her eyes focused on the ceiling. 'For five years.'

'When?'

'We split up five years ago.'

'You must have been ridiculously young when you got married.'

The words hurt. And angered. 'I was eighteen and maybe it seems ridiculous to you but I had my reasons. Don't presume to know me, because you don't.' And just as ridiculous were the tears that stung the backs of her eyes.

He immediately rolled towards her, then up onto an elbow, and looked deep down into her eyes. Further. All the way to her scarred heart. 'Hey...' he said softly. 'That's me being an insensitive jerk. I had no right to say that and I apologise.' He pressed a chaste warm kiss on her lips.

She stared up at him, seeing genuine concern. Because he was that kind of guy. He'd been blunt but he hadn't meant to hurt her. He'd just touched a particularly sensitive nerve. 'Apology accepted.'

He dipped his head so that his brow touched hers. 'It's just that I think of Lissa at eighteen. If she— Well.' He blew out a slow breath.

'Maybe you're too protective,' Sophie said carefully. 'Big brothers are like that sometimes.'

'What about your brother?'

'No.' She tried to remember the last time she'd seen him and couldn't. 'Corey's one of the exceptions.'

'So this man you married and divorced still puts clouds in your eyes. He still has the power to hurt you.'

'No.' She shook her head. 'How can a man who means nothing to you hold that kind of power? He has another woman, a young son and another baby on the way. He's happy. I'm happy,' she finished, determined, as much to convince herself as to convince Jared. If Glen was unfaithful to his current wife, Sophie didn't know about it. Didn't care.

'Do you want to tell me why you married him?'

'Because I was ridiculously young?' She gave a half-smile, forgiving Jared, and he reached for her nearest hand, twined his fingers with hers and somehow the story flowed like the river outside while she lay in his arms. She'd never shared her past. Only Pam knew her story, but sharing it with Jared felt natural, like lifting a burden off her shoulders. And it was almost as seductive as sex.

'My parents drank a lot and fought more. Dad was in and out of work. Violence was the norm. Corey was out of there by the time he was sixteen.

'But when *I* was sixteen Mum was involved in a major car accident and I stayed on to help. That lasted about eighteen months but eventually I couldn't stand the arguments and the booze any longer.

'I'd met Glen a few months earlier. He was ten years older than me and we were both working in hospitality. He seemed a good-natured guy and, looking back now, I guess I saw him as a substitute father.' A safe haven. A way out. 'One day we walked into a register office and just did it. When I informed my parents, they told me I was nothing but a disappointment, no better than my brother. Then they cracked open a cheap bottle of wine and began to drink themselves into their regular oblivion. I never saw them again.'

Jared gathered her to him. For a long moment he offered no words, just a hug as sweet and comfortable as it was uncomplicated.

'I send them Christmas and birthday cards with a cheque when I can afford it. They cash the cheques without fail but I've never heard boo from them. So I don't go back. I don't want to.'

He squeezed her hand. They both knew the money was wasted. 'So...you keep a dream diary,' he prompted, switching to a less painful topic a moment later.

'Yes.' Her pulse skipped a beat and she swivelled to face him. How did he know?

'I saw it on your bed when I left you in the shower. Hard to miss with the bright neon scrawl on the cover. Relax, Sophie, I didn't read it. I would never invade your privacy that way.'

'Okay.' She blew out a breath. Silence filled the tiny space between them and in those quiet heartbeats she trusted him with the truth. 'I used to have nightmares. My counsellor suggested it way back and it's become a routine.'

She felt the warmth of his understanding flow over her. 'Do you still have bad dreams?'

'Not so much now.' It occurred to her suddenly that she'd not made an entry since Saturday morning.

'Am I in there?' His voice turned playful.

She shoved at his arm. 'You know you are.'

'How many times?'

She grinned. 'Not telling.'

'What about fantasies, do you write them down too?'

'No. They're entirely different.'

'Tell me a fantasy.'

'I...can't.'

'Sure you can.'

'You'll laugh. Or think I'm awful.'

'I promise I won't do either.'

She snuggled nearer. 'I've always imagined making love in the open. Under the stars. I've never done it outside.'

'Never?'

She shook her head, then looked at him in the semi-darkness. 'You?'

The curve of his lips and the twinkle in his eyes pronounced him guilty but he didn't answer, just lifted her off the couch and carried her to his bed.

* * *

Jared's body clock woke him daily at precisely five-thirty a.m. no matter what time he'd gone to bed. Another of those predictable patterns that made up his life. He was also one of those people many either envied or hated for his ability to rise and shine the moment his eyes opened. He habitually swam for thirty minutes then breakfasted on oranges or pineapple, two eggs and strong black coffee.

But it had been a very long time since he'd woken with a woman lying beside him.

And that woman was currently dead to the world. And no wonder—he'd kept her awake most of the night. He'd not been able to get enough of her. Her sweet taste, her summer fragrance, her silken hair rippling over his body in black waves when she was on top. The moans she made when she came… and there'd been a few, he thought with a smile.

He wondered how long it had been since she'd been with a man.

She shifted in her sleep, a tiny smile touched the corner of her mouth as if she was dreaming. Of him and the things he'd done to her through the night, perhaps. The things they'd done to each other.

His erection hardened, throbbed, almost to the point of pain while he continued to watch her. But it was more than the physical. And that bothered him. Healthy lust was all well and good, but this…almost desperate need— *Scratch that thought.* Good grief, he was *not* desperate. But he'd never experienced anything quite like the way it was with Sophie. Alarming was what it was.

Sophie was moving on, and that was best for both of them. He reminded himself he went for outdoorsy girls—personal trainers rather than personal assistants.

And yet… He frowned, trying to make sense of it. They'd both agreed it was short term, so what the heck was the problem?

He needed space. Hardly daring to breathe, he backed off the bed and padded outside to where the pool's mirrored surface reflected the waning night.

Away from temptation. Better. He rubbed chilled arms then slid silently beneath the water. Cold water rushed past his ears as he torpedoed forward, feet and legs working economically. There *was no problem*, he assured himself as he broke the surface halfway down the pool's length.

Deliberately blanking his mind, he sliced through the water, concentrating on his body. The pull of his muscles, the drag of air into his lungs, the taste of chlorine on his lips. After some time, more relaxed and to keep himself that way, he mentally rehearsed the day ahead. They didn't have to be anywhere until their appointment at Brett Cameron's office.

Brett was refurbishing an apartment block in Noosa Heads overlooking the ocean. He'd used Jared's services for one of his resorts in nearby Mooloolaba. A man with a well-known business reputation and seemingly limitless funds.

But it wasn't only his reputation in business, his reputation with women was even more legendary. He was one of the wealthiest playboys this side of Brisbane.

And that was a problem.

Jared dragged himself to the edge of the pool and watched the eastern sky's pearl-grey dawn lighten. He and Sophie hadn't discussed exclusivity. Well, of course they hadn't. Why would they? A couple of weeks of fun, nothing to get serious or heavy about.

Brett Cameron wasn't Sophie's type, Jared assured himself. *And how the hell would he know that?* And even if he wasn't, every woman with a pulse was Cameron's type. Or so the rumours went.

Frowning, Jared padded to a tower of white shelves and helped himself to a towel, rubbed it over his head and face. Brett seemed a nice enough guy and Jared respected his business acumen, but where women were concerned...well, he was just glad he didn't have a daughter living in Noosa. A PA in Surfers Paradise was enough of a worry.

Deliberately, he shook it off and turned his thoughts to the present, swiping his body while he considered whether to let Sophie sleep or wake her. That feeling of desperation, of not being in control, washed through him once more.

No. He wasn't going to allow himself to be led down that path. Not by Sophie Buchanan, not by anyone. He tossed the towel over a lounger. After so many years of being there for his sisters, particularly Lissa, lust and good times were his due. He wasn't ready for anything more.

But… He paused on his way to the shower. He'd make something of the time they had left so that when they went their separate ways they'd both have something to remember.

CHAPTER ELEVEN

WAS that wonderful smell hot coffee? Sophie surfaced from sleep just enough to reach for Jared with her eyes still closed. To feel that hot male body next to her and make sure it wasn't a dream this time. But the sheets were cool and she realised she was alone. When she opened her eyes the sun was streaming through the window and sparkling on the surface of the pool outside.

She checked the time and bolted upright. Cripes, she'd slept in. They had a meeting in just over half an hour. Why had Jared not woken her? If she didn't know better she'd have thought he was deliberately leaving her behind, except she also knew he had a firm policy on not allowing pleasure to interfere with business. He'd expect his PA to be ready on time, no matter what her personal circumstances. Pam could attest to that. So was it some kind of test?

She scrambled out of bed and dragged the sheet around her like a toga since her clothes were in another bedroom and she was not going to wander the corridor naked. He was probably busy with last-minute details and just expected her to be ready…yikes…any minute now. Clutching the sheet, she made a dash to her room, grabbed her toiletries and flew into the shower.

Ten minutes later, a record by any woman's standards, she figured, dressed, minimum make-up, hair knotted severely beneath its clasp to mask its untamed nature since she'd not had time to wash it, she walked smartly into the kitchen area as if she weren't half an hour later than she ought to be.

She started to greet him, then stopped, suddenly self-conscious. What did you say to a new lover you'd had sex with all night long? A man who'd seen almost every inch of her body up close and personal. This was her second time at facing him after sex and she really needed to get used to it, but still, a flush rose up her neck. She was hardly an expert on such etiquette. *Just call me Ms Naïvety.*

He was sitting at a polished wooden table, the only furniture in the room that wasn't white, frowning over something on his laptop, but he looked up as she came to a stop by the coffee maker.

The residual heat she saw in his eyes was enough to light her fire all over again. But that was the only remnant of last night's passion and it flickered and died as he said, 'Good morning, Sophie.'

She thought of the impatient growl when he'd murmured her name against her breast last night. When he'd come deep inside her in the early hours. A contrast to this morning's briskly delivered greeting. And in the harsher, more demanding light of day it wasn't her lover she saw, but her boss. He was dressed for their upcoming appointments, his suit jacket on the sofa nearby. Freshly showered and shaved, he looked a picture of urban success and sophistication.

'Good morning.' She ran a finger inside the waistband of her slimline skirt and adjusted it, tucked a wayward strand of hair behind her ear and hoped she scrubbed up as well as he.

That she could be as sophisticated about last night as he.

Because he didn't mention it. Not a word, not even a hint, for goodness' sake… How awkward. No wonder they said office affairs were mistakes. She turned away, poured herself a mug of coffee and had only taken the first sip when Jared informed her they were leaving in five.

Fine. Be a pain in the proverbial. 'Okay.' She set her mug on the bench with a sharp *chink*. 'I'll get my stuff.'

She was tempted, so tempted, to demand he tell her what his problem was, but they had no time to spare and she didn't want to get into something they might have to stop in the middle of, which in turn could make the situation even more awkward.

Later, *after hours*, they were going to have a conversation about this. What did he think—that she was going to jump his bones in front of the client? That she didn't know what the word *professional* meant?

Or that he'd changed his mind and one night was enough.

An iron band tightened around her stomach. *Please, not that.* She knew they only had a short time but she wasn't ready to let him go yet. She wanted more. She needed to get him out of her system before she left Australia.

Jared turned the car radio's volume up and scowled at the road in front of them as they covered the few minutes it took to drive to their destination. He hadn't given Sophie time to eat breakfast. He should've woken her. His idea to go to the meeting without his PA was unprofessional. His usual clarity of mind was this morning a jumble of confusion. She was getting to him in ways that weren't supposed to happen. Making him indecisive. Making him look a complete incompetent.

Cameron met them at the front of the building. With his dark surfer-streaked gold hair and ocean-blue eyes, even Jared could see why women would find him attractive. He introduced Sophie.

'Welcome to Noosa, Sophie.' He shook her hand. 'You're a new member of Jared's team?'

'Just filling in for Pam for a few days.' She looked about her, took out a small pad and pen in favour of high tech. 'You have a lovely position here. Great potential.'

'I reckon so. I want Jared's opinion on it.'

Jared nodded. 'Okay, let's take a look around outside first and get a feel for the place.'

Perched on the hillside with breathtaking views of the beach and ocean, it had definite potential. Jared noted that Sophie returned their host's casual charm with a smile and professional courtesy as they inspected the premises. Jotting notes, asking pertinent questions of the two of them. If she found Cameron irresistible, she showed absolutely no sign.

On the other hand, neither did she show any sign that she found Jared even the tiniest bit irresistible. Busy with her notes, she barely acknowledged him at all, unless it was to clarify something, and then she did so with politeness and professionalism.

As it bloody well should be. Exactly what he expected, no, *demanded* of his PA. Why the hell should this time be any different?

Downstairs in a makeshift office, she set up her laptop on a small desk and worked on her own while Jared and Brett discussed the proposal and possible contractors.

Over coffee, she asked a question of Cameron. He leaned over to study her screen and met her eyes as he spoke. Sophie seemed to be riveted to her chair, those big amber eyes of hers looking up at him.

And Jared felt something uneasy and unfamiliar scratch across his skin and bury itself in his solar plexus like a hot blunt knife. The scrape and burn of possessiveness.

'What's your opinion, Jared?'

Jared blinked, aware they were both watching him and expecting some sort of reply. Sophie raised her eyebrows at him.

'Jared was only talking about that yesterday on the way up,' she said smoothly. 'Didn't you say you preferred to use local labour where possible?'

'Yes,' he replied. *What's your problem?* her expression said. He wished to hell he knew. *Thank you,* was his wordless reply. He shifted his gaze to his client. 'Did you have someone in mind…?'

When they were leaving, Cameron turned to Sophie and said, 'If you're looking for work and want something more permanent, my organisation has a vacancy at present. I'm sure you'd fill it more than adequately.'

His organisation? Not bloody likely, Jared thought. If she decided to stay, she'd be staying at Sanderson's.

Did she hesitate? He wasn't sure, but his breath caught in his chest. Then she smiled up at the other man. 'Thanks, but I'm going overseas soon.' Jared's relief, and a certain smugness, was short-lived.

'When you return…' Cameron pulled out a business card '…the offer will still be valid.' He wrote something on the back then handed it to her, trademark blue eyes twinkling. 'If circumstances change…'

Jared frowned. Was that an invitation in his tone? Was it business? Was it social? Was it pertinent to the message on the card? Damn it, from his position opposite Sophie he couldn't see what the guy had written.

Sophie glanced at the writing, smiled, nodded then tucked it into her purse. And then they were shaking hands. Smiles all round…

Paranoia. Jared clenched his fingers then very deliberately relaxed them. He extended his hand the moment Cameron relinquished Sophie's. 'Brett. Thank you for thinking of Sanderson's. You can expect our written proposal by next Wednesday.'

Cameron nodded, his grip firm. 'Look forward to it.'

Sophie wandered the Noosa Marina with Jared late that afternoon. Lots of cool blue—blue sails, blue paint, blue sky. There was a casual holiday atmosphere with tourists and locals alike eating at the variety of local cafés on the wharf, strolling the decking, poking around the one-of-a-kind stores from high-end fashion to fishing tackle.

Jared had suggested it as a good place to unwind after a

day's work and he was right. Trouble was, Sophie noticed, he never seemed to completely switch off. Not healthy.

The strong smell of the water pervaded the aroma of fresh-cooked seafood and the exotic fragrances emanating from the local day-spa shop. She rubbed a slight stiffness at the base of her skull as they passed the open door.

'Did I work you too hard today?'

She dropped her hand from her neck, shook her head. 'But I'd kill for one of those day-spa pampering packages.'

'According to Crystal, they're heaven-sent.'

'Actually I've never had one.' Sophie shrugged. 'The money never seems to stretch that far. But it's definitely on my to-do list.'

'Good idea.'

'Yes.' She glanced at him. 'They're good for men too, you know.'

His response was a mere rumble that sounded suspiciously like disagreement. Typical macho man.

There was a band playing in one of the restaurants; the wooden decking vibrated with the sounds of countless feet. A plethora of boats bobbed on the water; ferries and cruising restaurants all jostling for space in the popular marina, their gentle putter and the sound of water washing against their hulls filling the air.

Jared slowed as they approached a small cruiser tied up at the jetty, its paintwork gleaming red-gold in the late afternoon sun. A sunset dinner cruise by the looks of it, Sophie thought, admiring the little white-cloth-covered tables on board.

'You like sunsets and tonight looks like we might be in for a good one. How would you like to see it over the water tonight?'

'I'd love to. But if you're thinking this boat, it doesn't look like it's ready to sail for a while. There's no one else here. And you probably have to book.'

'Let's see.' Jared walked to the gangway where one of the

crew, dressed in whites, was laying out cutlery on one of the tables.

He looked up as they approached. 'Good evening.'

'Good evening.' Jared nodded to him. 'I made a booking earlier.'

The guy smiled. 'Mr Sanderson?'

'Yes.' Jared turned to Sophie. 'Feeling hungry yet?'

Her stomach fluttered but it wasn't with hunger. He'd remembered a throwaway comment she'd made last week about sunsets. Macho *and* romantic was Jared Sanderson. And she had the perfect dress to wear—a soft floaty sea/tea green that she'd popped in her bag at the last moment…back at their house. Right now her navy skirt and cream blouse were limp with a day's wear and humidity. 'Now?'

'Why not?'

'I'm in my work gear…and I've been in it all day. I'm hardly dressed for eating out.'

His gaze smouldered down her body like slow-moving lava. She'd never get used to that look and how it made her feel. Desired, dreamy, distracted.

Hot.

'Relax, Ms Buchanan, it's just you and me and a couple of crew. And you look as fresh as you did at ten o'clock.' He held out his hand to her, palm up. 'What do you say, is it all aboard?'

'And anchors away.' She had to smile because who could resist that roguish grin? Those scorching eyes? She laid her palm on his.

A cool breeze drifted across the river. They stood on the tiny deck upstairs and drank pink champagne from tall crystal flutes. She discovered a wild hibiscus flower in syrup at the bottom and enjoyed its delicious raspberry and rhubarb flavour on her tongue almost as much as she enjoyed the kiss Jared gave her the moment they were alone.

The aroma of roasting garlic and other herbs whetted their

appetites as they watched a gold-rimmed orange fireball sink below the bruised horizon. Within seconds the jagged slices of black and gold glinting on the water faded to a muted charcoal.

Moments later they returned to their table below, where a basket of steaming rolls awaited them.

'That was beautiful,' Sophie murmured. 'There's nothing quite like a tropical sun sliding into the water.'

'And you want to leave it all behind for cold, grey London smog.'

'It's not all smog.' She allowed the waiter to lay a napkin across her lap and admitted, 'But I am going to miss the tropics.'

'So what's at the top of your London to-do list?'

'All the traditional must-see places. But especially the Victoria Memorial in front of Buckingham Palace. I had a painting of it when I was a little girl. It was so whimsical and caught my imagination. You've been to London, I suppose.'

'No. Not yet. Don't even have a passport.'

'Oh?' Then she remembered he'd been guardian to his sisters his entire adult life, had focused on responsibility rather than his own pleasures, and nodded. 'You'll have to visit sometime.'

His eyes lingered on hers. 'Maybe I will.'

Confusion stole through her and she turned away and said, 'I can't wait to see that statue with its gold and marble and magical winged beings. And Queen Victoria in the midst of it all. I'll stand there and know that I've finally achieved my goal.'

She reached for her topped-up glass and took a liberal gulp while she studied the thin strip of land between water and fading aquamarine sky. The conical and distinctive volcanic shape of the distant Glasshouse Mountains on the horizon.

For the first time since she'd met Jared, she questioned her motivation for leaving. Did she have to leave everyone she knew and travel to the other side of the world for a change in scenery?

No. But she focused on what her head was telling her, not what her heart and emotions were saying. She wanted this trip. She'd wanted it for as long as she could remember. If she didn't go, she'd regret it.

And she wasn't going to change anything for a man. Not even a man she was falling for. Especially not for a man she was falling for. Going to the UK was the *best* thing she could do. For herself. And for Jared.

The main course arrived. Sophie chose salmon fillets on a bed of mashed potato with coriander, ginger and lime dressing, served with asparagus spears. Jared enjoyed a rare fillet steak with mushroom sauce and a selection of vegetables. It was a magnificent feast after the simple budget meals she'd been living on.

They ate for several minutes without talking. Just listening to the boat's motor, the swish of water against the hull.

'What about the people?' Jared said, scraping his fork over the bottom of his plate.

'People?'

'You said you'd miss the tropical climate.'

'Oh, yes, I'll miss the people too. I've got friends here.' She slid the last mouthful of salmon between her lips while she watched Jared and found she couldn't read his eyes now, at all. No matter how gorgeous he was or how much he was coming to mean to her... For the first time, she wavered. Then she pushed it away and said, 'But I'm not changing my mind.'

He watched her a moment, then set his cutlery on his empty plate, pushed it aside and leaned close so that his eyes reflected hers in the flickering candlelight. 'In that case we'll have to make the most of the time we have left.' His tone was low, rough and full of promise. And hypnotic. Like his gaze.

Everything around them seemed to fade out until all she was aware of was his intensity. From his eyes with their dark-rimmed irises that seemed to draw her into their depths, to the electric, almost mesmerising touch of his hand as it stroked her knuckles.

Drowning. 'Yes. Yes, we will.'

Her answer seemed to shake off the dreamy well they found themselves in and the look he gave her could only be interpreted as sinful determination. 'We'll return to the marina,' he said, gesturing the waiter hovering nearby over. 'Is that okay with you?'

'Very okay.'

There was still time to eat the dessert—fresh mango vanilla ice cream on an individual pavlova base—and enjoy a coffee before the boat pulled up alongside its berth.

Jared had plans for the rest of the evening. On the outside he maintained the cool, calm business façade he'd worn since this morning, but inside he was a bundle of firelighters ready for that first strike of the match. The way he'd been all day. The way he'd been every day since Sophie Buchanan had walked into his office.

He couldn't wait to feel her soft, summer-scented flesh against his again. Soon, very soon, he'd be burying himself inside her hot slippery centre. Easing the ache. Satisfying his need. Again and again, over and over, until he'd sated this all-consuming lust…

Because that was all it was. Wasn't it?

He tightened his grip on the wheel as they drove back to the house. That was all he'd allow it to be. She was leaving for London. But he hoped she'd remember this evening fondly and think of him.

The garage door rolled up, he slid into the parking spot, killed the engine and they both climbed out. He rounded the car, took her hand. 'There's something I want to show you before we go inside.' He led her to an enclosed garden at the side of the house, where a patch of velvety lawn bordered a garden of tea roses and the air was heavy with the scent of rich earth and the river.

And watched her jaw drop, her eyes widen in the soft light. It warmed him all the way through.

Sophie stared, unable to believe her eyes. A quilted throw lay on the lawn. A bottle of champagne chilled in a silver ice bucket alongside a cute terracotta pot crammed with cream roses. The scene was lit by a couple of Moroccan lamps, their intricate filigree silhouetted against the candle's warm glow. 'What's all this?'

'Jared Sanderson, at your service.' She turned her gaze on him and he smiled at her. 'You wanted to make love under the stars? Well, here we are.' He glanced up, waved a hand. 'Complete privacy under the Southern Cross at moonrise. Couldn't have asked for a better night.'

Oh. It looked like something out of a movie and her heart rolled over in her chest. 'But how?' she whispered. 'When…?'

'Magic. Aided by a little modern technology called a phone.' Jared stepped to her, turned her in his arms. The lamp glow sheened her skin. Her feminine fragrance drifted to his nostrils. He wanted slow and dreamy, but the sight of her, almost ethereal in the glow, nearly undid him. He tugged her down with him onto the quilt.

And while he popped the cork and poured the fizzy liquid into two crystal glasses, she gathered the roses to her nose. 'And chocolates…' She set the blooms down to grab the box, rip off the cellophane and pluck one out. 'This is like a dream.'

'So it is.' He felt the smile touch his lips, then his heart, as he offered her a glass, raised his own and clinked it to hers. 'To dreams.'

'To dreams.' She raised the crystal flute, took a sip, then lifted a chocolate to his lips. 'Share.'

He bit off half and his mouth flooded with caramel while she popped the remainder into her mouth and their gazes meshed and held. Even as she slid slowly down onto the quilt.

'Tonight I want to watch you come.' He saw her eyes widen, darken and for a few erratic heartbeats he gazed down at the vision sprawled beneath him. Her skin was flushed, as if she had a fever, a fever that put blooming roses in her cheeks and an extra spark in her eyes.

Then she was reaching for him and he followed her down and she had her hands in his hair, her fingertips scoring his scalp. And that spark in her eyes was a luminous topaz as she wrapped her hands behind his head and yanked him closer and murmured, 'So what are we waiting for?' against his lips.

His mouth dropped onto hers and his tongue plunged inside to savour her soft, full lips, her rich, dark drugging taste, so potent he felt light-headed with it.

Deliberately, he slowed his movements, cruising a hand over her knee, her outer thigh, then the tender inside of her leg and up…to find the barrier over her feminine hot spot already damp. For him. The knowledge vibrated through his body.

He lifted his mouth to trace a path over her jaw, to nibble his way down her neck, over her breast. To push her bra out of the way and roll her nipple between his lips. To taste its salty sweetness on his tongue and hear her suck in a sharp breath between her teeth while her restless fingers plucked at his hair and shoulders.

He could feel her heart galloping against his fingers and he wondered if she could hear his own. Because he'd never known it to beat this way before. This strange achy, urgent way that made him feel as if he were being pulled in opposite directions.

Shaking the confusing feeling away, he slid his fingers around her torso and unsnapped her bra. 'Let's lose the clothes.'

'Yes.'

He tugged her up onto her feet so that they stood toe to toe.

He stripped off his shirt, tossed it behind him while he watched her slip out of her blouse. Pull off her bra. Shimmy skirt and panties over her hips and down those amazingly long legs.

His blood pulsed through his body, throbbed in his erection, pounded low and insistent in his ears. She left him spellbound. He forgot to draw breath. Forgot to move until she reached out, undid his trousers with quick fingers and shoved them to his ankles. His boxers next. He stepped out of them, kicked them away. Then he realised the rest of her had followed her hands to the floor and was crouched in front of him.

She looked up and met his eyes and the message he read there... If he hadn't been transfixed to the spot, he swore he'd have stumbled. Then she reached out, her fingertips tracing his calves ever so gently, drawing circles on the backs of his knees, over his thighs...

Then, by God... Her face, her lips, a murmur away from his aching erection. He could feel her breath, a sweet torture on his burning flesh. His legs quivered. He fisted his hands in her hair as much for support as to stop her. Because if she touched him there, now, he'd explode... And as tempting as that was, it just wouldn't be fair.

'Sophie...' His hands still in her hair, he dragged her up against him until they were eye to eye. 'Later,' was all he said as he tumbled her back onto the quilt.

CHAPTER TWELVE

'I NEVER want to move again.' Sophie was tucked against Jared's shoulder in the main bedroom now, watching the play of light from the pool's reflection on the ceiling.

'Not even for ice cream?'

'Nope. I'm perfectly satisfied just as I am. You bought ice cream?'

'Yup.'

'Hmm.' They'd made love outside under the Southern Cross, then inside on top of the white silk quilt cover. They'd taken a shower and he'd seduced her again under the warm fragrant spray. She was well and truly satisfied. She didn't want to think about tomorrow, or next week. Or next month.

'But, oh, ye of great stamina,' she murmured, making an effort to lift one finger, slide its nail over a hard pectoral muscle and feel him shiver. 'If you're so inclined, I wouldn't object to you feeding me ice cream.'

'Not in the bedroom. You have to eat it in the kitchen—'

'Pfft. You sound just like—' *A father.* 'A big brother. A big, bossy brother.' Then because an image of him playing the daddy role threw her thoughts into disarray, she said, 'Do you treat all your girlfriends like they're kids?'

'I was going to say you have to eat it in the kitchen *naked*. Blackberry ripple? Your dream fantasy? Okay,' he continued when she pressed her lips together and didn't respond. He rolled onto his side and studied her curiously. 'All my girlfriends?'

Sophie felt her skin heat and wished the words unsaid. 'Pam

said you attend staff functions with a different girl every time, so I just assumed...'

Still watching her, he raised his brows as if it had never occurred to him that his trusted PA liked to gossip. 'Pam's got it wrong.'

Who did Sophie believe? Could she ever trust a man's word again? 'So you don't attend functions with a different girl each time?'

'Yes. No. Probably. Hell, I don't remember. It's not important enough.' He blew out an impatient breath and rolled onto his back once more. 'I'm no Casanova, Sophie, if that's what you think. I haven't got the time for it.'

She regretted her words. Even as a lover, she had no rights where he was concerned. Their relationship was temporary. She'd be gone soon and he'd be a memory.

'You've never had someone special? Someone you might have dated more than once?'

His answer was a while coming. 'Bianca. But she was a long time ago.'

'Tell me about her.'

'Why? She's in the past.'

'I told you about Glen. Were you in love with her?'

'In love?' Flicking her a glance, he said the words as if they were in a foreign language. 'We were too different,' he said at last.

Sophie wanted to know what had made him decide Bianca wasn't right for him. What was Jared's ideal woman and what kind of partner would he want on a permanent basis? 'Why were you attracted to her? How were you different? What made you change your mind?'

He looked at her again, eyes glittering in the dimness, and she was glad of the shadows. 'So many questions, Sophie?'

'I'm just curious.' She shrugged beneath his scrutiny as if it didn't matter. As if she didn't care. 'I like to understand people, that's all. No big deal.'

'Just curious, eh?'

She heard that familiar pumped male ego in his lazy tone. He scratched his chest with his free hand and she wanted to hit him.

She watched his profile as he stuck his arm beneath his head and looked up at the ceiling. 'We were the same in lots of ways. We both loved the outdoors and enjoyed the same activities. But when it came right down to it, she didn't want a kid interrupting the life she'd already mapped out for the two of us. And I couldn't live with that.'

The way he coupled himself with the faceless woman made Sophie's stomach clench. But the reason his relationship with Bianca hadn't worked out was the same reason he'd never want long term with Sophie.

No kids wasn't an option for Jared.

The back of Sophie's throat, her eyes, burned with the sting of unshed tears. Low in her belly the eternal aching emptiness unfurled, then twisted in on itself. She didn't have what a man—any man—wanted in a wife. She didn't have what it took to be the woman Jared would eventually marry. And he would marry down the track a bit, she knew. If what Pam said was true, he might be Playboy of the Gold Coast right now, but he was the marrying kind, a family guy.

It wouldn't be her he'd settle down with. Because she could never give him the babies she knew would be a non-negotiable part of any commitment.

Desperate to change the mood, to put some space between them, she sat up, reached for her plain cotton dressing gown with the pink polka dots on the wicker chair by the bed. 'Tell you what, I've changed my mind. I've decided I *can* move after all, and I want ice cream. In the kitchen. *Not* naked.'

Right now she couldn't be naked and be with him at the same time. Pulling on her dressing gown and hugging it around her like a security blanket, she headed down the hallway, her feet silent on the marble tiles. If he made a move on her any time soon she'd probably lose what little composure she had left, and she would *not* allow him to see that.

She set a couple of bowls on the counter top, pulled the tub of ice cream from the freezer. She'd just had a timely reminder that her life's path lay in a different direction from his.

A path she'd chosen. A path she'd wanted for a long time. She was jetting thousands of kilometres across the world. Independent. Living her dream.

Strange how it suddenly didn't sound half as exciting as it had a few days ago.

'Okay, not naked.'

At the sound of Jared's voice, Sophie turned to see him not naked too. He wore his boxers and a serious expression that asked too many hard questions. About the way she'd escaped from their bed so quickly.

Lose the angst fast, Sophie. She dipped her finger in the ice cream and licked its cold creamy-tart taste. 'It's good.'

'It's blackberry.' His eyes had that familiar wicked glint.

'I noticed.' She dipped her finger in again, held the blob to Jared's lips. *Keep things bright.*

They watched each other as he sucked it off her fingertip, but he was attuned enough to her mood to say, 'Let's sit somewhere comfortable and you can tell me what you think of this place.'

Changing the topic to something neutral, switching the focus away from her. She was surprised how sensitive he was to her emotions. Maybe because he was surrounded by females. Growing up with two sisters, a female dog and now a niece, he probably knew women better than she did herself.

They stretched out on the sofa, their legs close, their feet on the coffee table in front of them and their bowls of ice cream on their stomachs.

'You've bought yourself a new home in Surfers to renovate, Pam told me.'

'Yes, but I'm in no hurry. That's why we're staying here. I like some of the ideas and I wanted a close-up inspection.'

'So what do you like about it?' Sophie asked, sucking on her spoon.

'The pool outside the bedroom, for starters. I can sleep, swim, then breakfast in one fluid sequence.'

'It's a very dangerous idea with young children around,' she pointed out.

He turned to her, his eyes probing hers before saying, 'I don't have any children.'

Not yet. 'What about Arabella? When she comes to visit? In a year she'll probably be walking and getting up to no end of mischief.'

He frowned, tapping his spoon pensively against his bowl. 'Good point. I hadn't thought of that. Thank you.'

'Other than that, though, the pool's a splendid idea.'

'Any other thoughts on the place?'

'I like that it's so light and airy you feel as if you're outdoors. And the open-air kitchen that's not really a kitchen but more of an island.'

'Speaking of feeling as if you're outdoors...' he reached for her bowl, set it on the coffee table with his '...there's an architectural wonder in the master bedroom I haven't shown you yet.'

And a wonder it was indeed.

Long after Jared had fallen asleep, Sophie was still staring up at the field of stars visible through the massive circular window. With a flick of a switch it could be cleverly concealed by a ceiling panel in the form of a rosette. Amongst the snowy pillows it was like lying on top of a cloud and watching the night drift past. Like magic.

And hadn't these last few days been magic? she thought on a sigh. One magic moment after another with the man of her dreams. Literally.

The man she'd fallen in love with.

Yes. She'd fallen in love with Jared, and perhaps it was the most magic thing of all that she could allow herself that luxury.

But magic wasn't real; it was an illusion and it didn't last. And Sophie knew, with a heart that was already breaking apart, that very soon the magic would end.

'I've got another job for you, if you'd like it,' Jared told Sophie late the next afternoon. They'd arrived back at the office after lunch and were going over some work that had accumulated in their absence. Pam would be back on board on Monday and Jared knew Sophie could do with the extra money.

She looked up from the folder she was studying. 'What kind of work?'

'I promised Melissa an eighteenth birthday party. I've been too busy to make a time with her to organise it. If you could meet with her, make and oversee the arrangements, I'll continue paying you what you're making now until the night of the party. You probably have more idea what she wants than I do anyway.'

Her expression brightened, but then a little frown creased her brow. 'When were you planning it for? I'm leaving in a couple of weeks, remember.'

He remembered. And the knowledge was like a grass seed in his sock. A minor but constant niggle. If he'd been a less focused man he might have said to hell with the paperwork and spent what was left of the afternoon in Sophie's bed. He really was in danger of turning into an indulgent and irresponsible idiot.

He reached for a business card, jotted Melissa's contact details on the back. 'It'll fit in well, then. It's two weekends from now.'

'Two weeks on my current pay? To organise a party? That's… generous…thank you.'

'You're helping me out, so thank *you*.' He slid the card across the desk. 'I'll leave it to you to contact Melissa. I've already set up a credit card. It'll be available Monday, spend whatever you need.'

'Okay… It sounds like fun.' She shifted forward on her chair. 'I'll just sort these and make sure everything's ready for your efficient PA's return before I leave.'

'She'll appreciate it.' All business, he noted as Sophie stood, shuffled the folders on his desk into a neat little pile. He and Sophie worked well as a team. Understood each other. Respected each other. They could be professional when required.

And he could have her naked on his desk in five seconds flat.

His imagination slammed into overdrive and its very lack of that professionalism was its own appeal. His body tightened. Blood thickened and throbbed in his groin. It was five-thirty on a Friday afternoon. Those employees who hadn't yet left for their weekend were drinking up a storm in the staff lounge—he could hear the laughter and clink of glass, the muted hum of a middle-of-the-road CD.

No one was going to come looking for workaholic Jared.

He stood too, stepped around to the side of his desk. *Lock the door, close the blinds. For once, do what no one expects of Jared Sanderson.* 'Sophie…' He could barely recognise his own husky voice. But he heard the possessive tone and the promise…

And he saw barely veiled humour flit across her expression as she backed up and crossed the room in record time. 'In your dreams, Mr Sanderson.' She poked her head around the door a few seconds later with a seductive sparkle in her eyes. 'My place, thirty minutes. Don't keep me waiting.'

He grinned, warnings to self about the dangers of indulgence and irresponsibility where Sophie was concerned already forgotten. 'I'll be there with wine.'

Still grinning, he returned to his chair. His lover and his

PA rolled into one generous, intelligent, talented package. He'd never have thought of his PA in that way. Then again, he'd never had a PA quite like Sophie. And it worked. With Sophie it worked.

They'd come into the office this afternoon as professionals, as equals. They'd been able to put aside the fact that they'd spent the past couple of nights bonking each other senseless. Difficult. Very difficult.

Shaking his head, he forced his attention back to work. What the hell, he decided, slapping his folder shut. He deserved an early finish.

The weekend flew by as quickly as their stay in Noosa had. Except that for the first time in as long as he could remember, Jared allowed no interruptions from the office to impinge on their time together. No emails, no text messages, no phone calls.

They walked touristy shopping malls and drank coffee, wandered the beach and watched surfers ride waves, took a leisurely drive and a picnic basket into the Hinterland where the air was cool and green.

He showed her some of the developments he'd overseen up and down the Gold Coast. The new apartment block in Broad Beach that he intended renovating and living in someday. He took her home to his place where she and Lissa got along as if they were best friends rather than recent acquaintances.

But he didn't stay the nights with her. In the early hours he left her warm comfort and went home. He knew his sister wasn't fooled, but it wasn't so much about Melissa as about himself. This way it was easier to remember that this…whatever it was that he had with Sophie wasn't serious. It was temporary. A fling with a rapidly approaching use-by date.

Just a fling, Sophie reminded herself as she woke up alone at seven a.m. She hadn't asked him to stay the night when he'd rolled out of bed and gone home around two a.m. for the last three mornings. *Because it was just a fling.* She touched a fingertip to the dent in the pillow where he'd lain. No point in getting used to waking up beside him. Cocooned in their shared musky warmth. Seeing his eyes darken with desire when he turned his head on the pillow and saw her watching.

Shaking it away, she dragged herself out of bed and pointed herself in the direction of the bathroom. She focused her thoughts on this morning. No doubt he was already at work and she was meeting Melissa and Enzo at Enzo's restaurant to plan Melissa's birthday.

Enzo was waiting when she arrived. At this hour, the restaurant was closed to the public, but they sat at a table where a couple of floor-to-ceiling windows were thrown open to the salty sting of beach air. Early sunshine spilled onto the table and the aroma of croissants and coffee stirred her appetite.

While they waited for Melissa, Enzo poured coffee. 'So you're planning Melissa's party?'

'Yes.' She took a sip of the strong black brew. 'I know Jared would've preferred some fancy-schmancy event planner but Pam's back this week so Jared asked me if I'd like the job. Very kind of him since he knows I could do with the extra money. I'm going overseas.' She mentally frowned at the distinct lack of enthusiasm she heard in her last words. Of course she wanted to go overseas. She did.

Enzo nodded. 'Jared is a very kind man.'

'You've known him a long time?'

'He worked for Rico and Luigi a long time ago in the fish shop. I was fourteen at the time. Jared wanted to show he could support his sisters, bring in some money and study all at once.'

'That sounds like Jared. Who's Luigi? Another brother?'

Enzo shook his head. 'Rico loved him like a brother but he was, in fact, Rico's business partner. But Luigi was an evil man. My brother trusted Luigi but he fiddled the books, then absconded with all their money. Bankrupted Rico, put my restaurant into financial difficulties while I was trying to bail my brother out.'

She shook her head. 'That's horrible.'

'Jared came to our rescue. He was a rich man by then. Set Rico up in new premises. Gave us both financial backing. We owe him a great debt.'

'He's a pretty special guy.'

'He likes you. I can tell. Did you say you were going overseas?'

'Very soon.'

'Maybe you should reconsider. You don't want to let a good man like that get away.'

She felt a twitch of irritation between her shoulder blades but Enzo was a typical family-oriented Italian and she needed to remember that for Jared, too, family was everything. She pasted on a smile. 'I'm not trying to catch a guy, Enzo.'

His brows shot up. 'No? What about babies? A little Jared? Or a little Soph—'

'No.' She cut him off. The images he was conjuring jabbed at her heart. 'I'm—ah, Melissa's arrived.'

Enzo turned. 'Good morning, Melissa.'

'Good morning.' Melissa exchanged a quick sisterly kiss with Enzo then sat, smoothing her flyaway red hair behind her ears. 'I'm late. Sorry.' She beamed at Sophie. 'This is so exciting getting you to help me organise things. Perhaps we should let Enzo carry on with his own work while we come up with a few ideas first?'

'Good idea.'

'I'll let you two get on with it.' He poured Melissa a coffee. 'Give me a call when you're ready.'

'Mmm, smells heavenly. Thanks, Enzo. I have a few suggestions...' Melissa pulled out a notebook.

Sophie switched on her laptop. 'That's a good start.' She

could see a variety of quick and clever sketches as Melissa flipped through for the page she was looking for.

'Got it,' Melissa said finally, and reached into her bag for a pen. 'Ready.'

'Okay.' Sophie's fingers hovered over the keyboard. 'What kind of party were you thinking of?'

CHAPTER THIRTEEN

THE rest of the week passed in a flash for Sophie. She and Melissa had come up with plenty of ideas for Sophie to chase up, and, being virtually last minute, the invitations had to be printed and sent pronto. She wondered why Jared had left it so late—if it had been an idea he'd had on the spur of the moment or whether he'd been too busy and forgotten.

The evenings were spent together in her apartment, but sometimes if he finished work early they went out for dinner or caught a movie. He surprised her one night at a club where she discovered he was a pretty cool dancer.

One thing didn't change. They couldn't keep their hands off each other. Sometimes it was in a rush of heat and energy, at other times the mood was slow and lazy. Always both familiar and sparkling new. Always exciting.

She let her fun, flirtatious side fly and kept her darker emotions firmly bolted down. There'd be a time when she'd have to take them out and confront them, and that time loomed like a storm on the horizon.

The phone rang late on Saturday afternoon. According to Jared, Crystal and Ian were taking a well-deserved break and were having dinner out, Jared's treat. He was babysitting Arabella for a few hours and would see Sophie around eleven p.m.

Sophie was relieved that he hadn't asked her to join him at Crystal's place. She didn't want the ordeal of seeing baby Arabella again. Last night she and Jared had been to a concert in Brisbane and hadn't arrived home till after midnight. She'd spent the day sorting through stuff and packing and they had no definite plans for this evening.

So when the buzzer sounded around seven while Sophie was ironing, she was unprepared for the sight of Jared and baby Arabella at her front door.

He smiled at Sophie, and with Arabella tucked up against him, her tiny face over his heart, Sophie's own heart felt as if it were being squeezed in a vice. That was Sophie's favourite place too.

Stupid to be jealous of a baby. To be jealous of Jared because it was all so easy for him, so natural, so inevitable that he'd probably have his own baby in a few years and she'd *never have the chance*. Stupid to be so jealous she wanted to lash out at him for her own inadequacies. *Stupid, stupid, stupid.*

She bit her lip. She was *not* going to cry. Not in front of Jared. Never in front of Jared. He held a baby capsule in his free hand. Sophie did not offer to help. 'What are you doing here?'

'I couldn't get her to settle,' was his excuse. 'I thought a drive might help.'

Arabella's eyes were closed, the eyelids so fragile they were almost transparent. Sophie wanted to reach out and touch the silky, sweet-smelling skin. To snatch her away and cuddle her against her own breast. Over her own heart. 'She looks just fine to me.'

Looking away, Sophie walked back to her ironing task, leaving Jared to put the capsule down so that he could close the door.

'She is. *Now*,' he said, bringing baby and carrier to the sofa. 'The car's motion put her to sleep.'

'Great.' She smoothed a blouse over the ironing board. 'So what's the problem?'

'But she woke the moment I stopped,' he went on. 'So I've been walking up and down your street for the past fifteen minutes. She's just dropped off again but I've got a sneaky feeling she's going to wake up the moment I put her in her capsule and I only have one bottle of milk left.'

'Then don't.' *Please don't.* She didn't want to have to notice her. A newborn's cry set off emotions she didn't want to deal with. Especially not with Jared watching on.

'I have to, Sophie, so I can get her stuff out of the car. Unless you want to hold her?'

She picked up the iron, swiped it over the garment in front of her. 'Try putting her in her capsule first.'

'Didn't think so,' he murmured, almost to himself. He peeled Arabella off him with the greatest care and laid her in her carrier. She snuffled but didn't wake. 'I'll get her gear. Be back in a jiff.' Then he was gone.

And in the perverse way of things, Arabella woke at that moment with a snorting noise that quickly turned to hiccuping sobs and finally one piercing wail.

Sophie told herself the baby was perfectly safe, that the sound was normal baby noise. That Jared would be back any moment. She closed her eyes as another howl rent the air and tried to resist but…oh, it was like…telling your heart to stop beating.

When Sophie turned, the little face was scrunched up and red, her tiny fists were waving in the air. And, oh… It seemed… it seemed Sophie's legs had a will of their own.

She knelt beside the sofa, reached out a finger. Her heart thumped fast against her ribs. Everything inside her yearned. Just one touch… One touch of that petal skin… So smooth, so silky.

The moment Sophie stroked a finger down the infant's cheek, all noise ceased instantly and Arabella stared at her with barely focused eyes. For a beat out of time Sophie froze. Then she caressed her again. Leaned closer to smell that baby scent of powder and milk, to curve her palm over the soft fuzzy scalp.

And forgot she didn't go near babies.

'Hush little baby, don't you cry…' She sang the lyrics so quietly she barely heard herself. But Arabella heard. And she seemed entranced, her tiny mouth open, her eyes…Sophie swore they knew her.

No. She bit her lip to stop the tears. Why was fate so cruel? To give her such a gift and at the same time to take her ability to have babies away? It wasn't fair.

Yet she was still a woman, she reminded herself. Jared had shown her that. For the first time in five years he'd made her feel like a woman, feminine and desired and cherished.

But as she gazed down at the infant, the doubt demons perched on her shoulder. Would he still feel the same way if he knew? To be rejected again, to see the man she'd fallen in love with look at her as less…she didn't think she'd ever get over it.

Jared came to a halt inside the doorway. Sophie was leaning towards the baby capsule, her hand fisted against her mouth and a moment's alarm slid through him. 'Sophie?'

She whirled to him, eyes wide and panicked before she blanked the emotion and said, 'She seems to be settled now.'

He hadn't seen her touch the infant but he could've sworn he'd witnessed…something.

And in that blinding moment of clarity he'd seen his future flash before him.

A future that included Sophie. A home. And kids.

Home and kids? He wasn't near ready for any of that and shook his head to clear it. 'Sophie, wh—'

'I'm sorry to run out on you.' She glanced at her watch, then yanked the iron's cord from the wall socket and picked up a little black blouse from the ironing board. 'But I wasn't expecting you yet. I'm meeting friends for a drink this evening since you weren't coming by till eleven. Feel free to stay here for a while though…'

As long as you and the baby are gone when I get back. He

read those words in her expression as clear as glass, in the lack of eye contact, her jerky movements. 'You didn't say you were going out.'

'I'm not meeting a guy, if that's what you're thinking.'

'No,' he said carefully, 'that's not what I'm thinking.'

She held the blouse up and inspected it. 'I wasn't aware we had to account to each other for every moment of our time.'

No strings. Wasn't that the exact kind of relationship he wanted? *Damn it.* 'Is that what you think this is about, Sophie?'

'Jared.' Her fists tightened on the garment she held and now her eyes found his. Locked on his and pleaded with him. 'Let's just enjoy our last few days?' Her appeal was like a tangible presence in the room with them. 'Please?'

'Okay,' he said finally, the remnants of his vision of a future he'd never imagined fluttering like petals on the periphery of his consciousness. Hitching the baby bag onto his shoulder, he picked up the carry basket with its now cooing passenger. What choice did he have with an infant in his care for the next few hours? 'Go and enjoy your evening. I'll be back at eleven.'

As he turned to pull the door shut he saw her shoulders slump and her eyes held a puzzle he wished to hell he understood.

Twenty-three minutes past two. He should be doing what Sophie had asked and making the most of the rest of the night with her. Instead, he wandered the night-darkened esplanade, the eternal *thump-boom* of the surf in his ears, his thoughts going around in circles and coming back to what Sophie had said when he'd left earlier.

Ten days. Why let her obvious hang-ups with kids come between them and a good time? Live and love to the max, enjoy what they had while they had it. Wasn't that all that mattered in their 'short-term relationship'? That was obviously what mattered to Sophie.

And it was exactly what he'd told himself he wanted. She

wasn't looking for more either. So it was just about perfect, right?

Right. He turned back, following the sandy path back to his car. He ignored the hollow feeling in his gut as he slid onto the leather seat.

But he didn't switch the ignition on. Instead, he slammed his fists on the steering wheel. *No.* Not *right.* Nothing about this was right. Just good times?

The hell it was.

He stared through the windscreen but he wasn't looking at the ocean view. He was seeing Sophie leaning over the baby. Moreover, he wasn't seeing himself as only his sisters' guardian, he was seeing himself as a father in the truest sense of the word.

He shook his head. Wrong decade. Sophie wasn't the woman for him long term, she was all about adventure and discovering new places. As was her right, he told himself, and after what she'd been through, she deserved it. Who was he to interfere with her dreams and plans? Nor was this trip she was embarking on the end of the world. A few months. A year tops and she'd be back. He could almost guarantee it.

Over the week Sophie had brought sunshine and summer and sparkle to what he was only now realising had become an exceedingly dull existence.

He'd made love to her in the sea and watched the sense of humour spark in her eyes, made love to her in the centre of a macadamia plantation and watched the green reflected in the amber. He'd laughed more. Because he'd found more to laugh about with Sophie to share it with.

And every now and then he'd remember she was leaving and a shadow would steal over the sun.

He forked frustrated fingers through his hair. For the second time in his life he'd fallen for a woman. And this time he'd fallen hard. And these feelings he had were nothing like those he'd had for Bianca.

These feelings ran deep. So deep they touched his soul and he didn't know if he'd ever be free of them. And powerful enough to rock his world to its very foundation. It was nothing like he'd ever experienced—dangerously so.

Despite his deepening feelings, he wasn't prepared to compromise what he believed in or how he wanted to live his life for someone else's whims and fancies and ideals. Bianca hadn't fitted into the world he'd created for himself and his sisters, so Bianca was history. Simple.

With her outlook on life so different from his own, Sophie didn't fit into his world either. But something didn't gel and he couldn't put his finger on what it was. Whatever it was, it was far from simple.

Sunday morning. Sophie woke to daybreak's murky light stealing over her window sill, although she couldn't remember falling asleep. The last time she'd checked the time it had been ten past four. She'd resisted trying to contact Jared. He'd come when he was ready, and if he didn't… She had no one to blame but herself.

He hadn't come.

Sitting on the edge of her bed, she dragged on her dressing gown. Her eyes felt swollen and gritty, her nose was still blocked from her crying jag hours ago and there was an empty ache in her chest that wouldn't go away.

She had no idea whether it was over with Jared, why he hadn't turned up last night or what he was thinking. But rather than sitting around like a misery guts and moping about it, she had packing to do. The furniture belonged to the apartment but she needed to sort what she was taking with her, and toss or store the rest.

She could ring Jared…and apologise. She headed for the kitchen. She'd seen the disappointment in his eyes when she'd mentioned keeping tabs on one another. No, he'd come on his own terms or not at all.

She'd just made a pot of tea when he turned up. Leaning on the door frame with his darkly stubbled jaw, furrowed hair and bloodshot eyes, he looked as ragged and sleep-deprived as she felt.

He was just about the most beautiful sight she'd ever seen.

She stood back to let him enter. He smelled of the beach, cool morning air and impossible dreams. He closed the door behind him and they stared at each other for a long moment.

She couldn't read his expression but maybe she saw something that gave her hope? Courage? 'I missed you.' She hadn't meant to say them but the words tumbled out.

He didn't answer. Just wrapped one large hand around the back of her neck, hauled her face up to his and kissed her. Hard. Possessively and with a kind of angry passion.

She felt his strength in the rigid arm that supported her, in his rock-hard body as she melted against him. Perhaps some of that strength would flow into her…

But no. He released her with such speed and vehemence she almost stumbled. 'We need to cool it.' He shoved his hands in the back pockets of his jeans and shook his head, then watched the window where the pale sun slid through a smudge of grey. 'This has got way too intense and I sure as hell don't need it right now. Neither do you.'

He regretted that kiss and the loss of control. The knowledge was both painful and poignant for Sophie. But it was for the best and he was right, they needed to put some distance between them. In one week the man she loved would be a world-away-distant memory.

She wouldn't cancel her trip; she needed it, now more than ever. She wouldn't try to convince him that they could be more than short term. She wouldn't lay open her vulnerable heart and tell him the things she wanted to tell him—that she not only wanted to be his lover but his wife, the mother of those children he so obviously wanted and expected of a marriage…

She couldn't give him those children and she couldn't risk

seeing the light in his eyes dull to disappointment when she told him.

She should back off now, tell him it had been fun then pack up and go to Brisbane for the last week until her flight left from there, and never see him again.

But with the party next weekend, she couldn't let Melissa or Jared down now and Jared had paid her up front to do the job.

She'd never been a quitter, she told herself, ignoring the little voice saying, *Except where Jared's concerned.* And the thought of never seeing him again was too painful, what with him standing within touching distance, larger than life and twice as thrilling. Twice as precious.

'So what are you trying to say?' she asked his back. She didn't want to know. She had to know. Better to know now...

For the second time, he didn't answer her. Turning around, he didn't give her time to read his expression, just swept her into his arms and carried her towards the bedroom like an impatient man claiming what belonged to him...

They didn't talk at all, they made love. Tumultuous love-making of the deep and dark and desperate kind that satisfied the flesh but resolved nothing.

Jared didn't give her time to refuse or argue or demand. He wanted her now—all of her—heart, body and mind—all, and with an urgency he'd never known.

And she gave him everything. He felt it flow from her like a fast-flowing stream. Momentarily sweeping away those earlier doubts and questions on a tide of emotion he struggled to contain.

After, he held her trapped within his arms, breathing in the musky scent of their own creation. Revelled in the silken rain of ebony hair that cascaded over his shoulder and down his chest. His words had dried up like cockles in the sun. He couldn't remember a single one. One look at her when she'd opened the door all mussed and flushed and sleepy and all he could think was, *Home*. All he knew was that he wanted her. In every way. Whatever the cost. Whatever the sacrifice, whatever the risk.

But how would she respond if he opened his heart and told her? Would she be willing to make that sacrifice too, and take that risk with him? Was he even ready to find out?

CHAPTER FOURTEEN

ON THE following Saturday night Sophie put the finishing touches to her make-up and stood back to check her reflection. She'd chosen a sapphire-blue dress that left one shoulder bare and had an asymmetric hemline. But tonight wasn't about her, it was Melissa's big night.

The past week had been hectic. She'd stored what she wasn't taking. The rest spilled out of two open suitcases on her living-room floor.

The time had also given Sophie an opportunity to get better acquainted with Melissa. She was a complex girl but she obviously adored her big brother. It was just that, according to Lissa, she was feeling suffocated.

Sophie understood Melissa wanted to test her independence. Having a protective brother, while a wonderful thing, could prove stifling—or so Sophie imagined, thinking of her own long-lost sibling. Lissa wanted her own place and she'd said Jared needed his privacy too.

Sophie agreed. She added a pair of silver drop earrings to complete her look. But Melissa knew Sophie was leaving so why the conspiratorial smile when she'd mentioned his need for space? Did she think she and Jared were something more?

Did she maybe think Sophie was coming back sooner rather than later? Sophie stared at her eyes in the mirror. *No regrets, remember.*

She and Lissa had come to an arrangement. Lissa was taking over Sophie's apartment. The landlord was satisfied. Jared had accepted the inevitability with only minor reservations. Everyone was happy…except Sophie.

Oh, she *was* happy. She told herself so every day and smiled at her reflection to prove it. Who wouldn't be, with the trip of a lifetime so close she could almost smell it?

Because there was Jared.

Her smile slipped away, her heart contracted and a brief mist clouded her vision. Jared, with that adorable crease in his cheek and something deep in his eyes that told her he had secrets he wasn't going to share with her.

She was leaving and she knew he cared for her more than a little. His sister was moving out after she left and he'd be on his own for the first time. A man who loved having his family close and enjoyed companionship. Sophie wondered how he'd deal with that.

And he'd given her a most precious gift, a gift he wasn't even aware he'd given: her acceptance of self, belief in herself. So after consulting Melissa, and with Crystal's okay, Sophie had arranged a surprise she hoped he'd recognise for what it was and enjoy.

Even with Melissa planning to live independently, Jared was still very much his youngest sister's protector. Sophie remembered a conversation she'd had with Melissa.

'I guess that's because you're the baby,' Sophie had said. 'When your father died, Jared wanted to make sure you—'

'No.' Melissa shook her head. 'My father wanted nothing to do with me. I'm not his biological daughter. Our mum had an affair. He discovered it after she died. I was only a few weeks old, so I don't remember her.

'But I remember my father's coldness towards me and my bad behaviour as a result and getting attention for all the wrong reasons. I was alone, I was different, I was an outsider. I had no biological parents and only a half brother and sister and they had each other.'

Sophie touched Melissa's hand, sad that she couldn't see the blessing she'd been given in Jared. 'But, Melissa…'

'I know.' Melissa flapped a hand. 'I'm so lucky. Even as a four-year-old I remember Jared standing up to his father and copping a beating to protect me.'

'*Beating?*'

'Oh, yeah.'

Which sounded to Sophie as if it had happened more than once.

Melissa didn't want to hurt Jared's feelings by appearing ungrateful and moving out and leaving him all on his lonesome but she needed to do her own thing. She and Crystal were also very concerned about his work-life balance.

Yes, there were women, but not often and he never dated the same one more than a couple of times. He needed a woman who could light his fire, Melissa had said. And she'd looked at Sophie when she'd said it. A woman he could settle down with and make a family of his own.

Melissa worried he wasn't looking because he still felt that responsibility for his baby sister who was no longer a baby, but that he might see things differently if she wasn't around…

The apartment solution was a good one, Sophie thought, on the short cab journey to Enzo's. Jared had organised a taxi for Sophie ahead of time so she could ensure everything was organised and he was bringing Lissa. A place of her own would give Melissa independence, she'd be ten minutes away from Jared, and Pam lived in the same complex if she needed help.

And Jared could move on with his life.

And Sophie was *not* going to think about that tonight. She'd be much too busy making sure everyone else had a good time.

Jared shuffled Sophie around the makeshift dance floor to one of the local band's recent hits. The rhythm was essentially fast but they moved to their own beat—much slower and out of time if anybody cared enough to look.

The restaurant's sliding doors had been removed and the dance floor set up outside. Coloured lanterns danced on their strings in the gentle ocean breeze, the scents of kerosene torches and salty air and fried garlic assaulted the senses.

'You did a brilliant job getting it together on such short notice,' Jared said against her ear. 'You've worked practically non-stop and I appreciate it. Thank you.'

Sophie looked over his elegantly clad shoulder. Pam was in the corner having an up-close and serious conversation with some hotshot Sophie recognised from the office. Crystal and Ian had left earlier with Arabella, but the guest of honour was laughing up a storm with some of her friends by the remains of the birthday cake inside. 'You're very welcome and I'm grateful for the opportunity.'

Melissa had wanted the occasion to be a formal affair. All the guys looked gorgeous in suits despite the warm evening and the girls, glad of an excuse to tart themselves up for a change in what was normally a casual lifestyle, wore semi-formal dresses and plenty of bling.

Every one seemed to be having a good time. Sophie had enjoyed a champagne to celebrate the cake cutting. And Jared, as usual, looked irresistible in his dark suit and classy silver tie.

He must have noticed her smiling—or was she drooling?—because he tilted her face up to his, placed a slow melting kiss on her lips that promised all kinds of anticipated delights and murmured against her mouth, 'I think we can leave now.'

Oh, and she wanted that promise fulfilled. 'But it's only ten-thirty and the party's my responsibility. I need to—'

'Please the man who paid you,' he murmured again.

He slid one large finger beneath the strap on her right shoulder and drew a sensuous circle there. 'Ah…' She shivered at the little thrill of anticipation that trickled all the way down to her toes, but she had a job to do. 'But I...Lissa—'

'Will thank you very much for all you've done. Then she'll say goodnight and tell us to enjoy the rest of the evening.'

The way he said that, the way his eyes darkened, the way his finger slid lower, beneath the fabric of her dress and towards the top of her bra... That promise again... And the trickle became a torrent.

'These young things don't want us oldies hanging around.' He was already withdrawing his finger to take her hand and lead her towards Melissa to say their goodbyes.

Sophie laughed. 'You talk as if we're over the hill.'

'We are to them. Come on.'

And she knew why he was insisting they leave early. It was their last night together. Tomorrow afternoon she was flying to Sydney to catch her international flight scheduled for Monday morning.

Jared drove her home. Except...they didn't seem to be headed in that direction. 'Where are we going?'

'Wait and see.' Apartment buildings and luxury hotels twinkled with a million lights as they drove a short distance, then Jared pulled to a stop under the portico of a well-known five-star hotel.

'We're staying here?' She stared up at the gold and marble and glass.

'I thought we might.' His desire-darkened eyes burned into hers.

'All night.' They hadn't spent the night together since Noosa. She'd hated that, but now, with only this night left, maybe it was a very unwise idea. Maybe the most dangerous idea she could think of.

And far too seductive to refuse.

He seduced her further with the gentle brush of a fingertip over her lips. 'All night. We even have a late checkout in the morning.'

'But I didn't bring—'

He leaned across the centre console and nuzzled the underside of her jaw. 'Believe me, you won't need a thing.' When he straightened again, her pulse was already leaping in anticipation.

'But tomorrow morning...'

'Got it sorted...' He pulled a small bag from behind his seat and set it on her lap. 'Pam packed a few things. She hoped you wouldn't mind her using her spare key for your apartment without your permission.'

'Oh, Pamela, Pamela...you're in on this too?' She pressed her hands to her flushed cheeks. They'd organised this behind her back. Pam hadn't breathed a word at the party. Not a look. Not even a glimmer.

'Okay?'

She nodded, struggling not to feel overwhelmed. 'Okay.'

A woman met them in the lobby. She wore a baby-pink shirt, smelled of sandalwood and exuded serenity. She smiled a somewhat conspiratorial welcome at Jared, then turned her smile on Sophie. 'Good evening, Sophie.'

'Good evening.' When the woman indicated she should follow her, Sophie looked to Jared. 'What's happening?'

'A thank-you for your effort on Lissa's behalf, and mine, these past couple of weeks. You wanted a day-spa package. You've got a night-spa one instead.'

'Oh, I...'

'I'll be waiting when you're done. Thanks for this, Aimee. I owe you one.' He nodded to the woman, then kissed Sophie lightly on the cheek. 'Enjoy.'

And Sophie spent the next hour and a half in the hotel's Wellness centre being treated like a celebrity by two—yes, *two*—therapists. The popular Goddess facial. A de-stress and aromatherapy massage. Chakra balancing. Mineral salt scrub and manicure.

She was pampered within an inch of her life.

When she was done Aimee gave her a luxuriously soft towelling robe embroidered with the hotel's logo to put on and showed her to a private elevator that led to a penthouse suite. She should be tired but she'd never felt more alive.

When Sophie had stepped inside the lift, Aimee pressed the button and smiled. 'Enjoy your evening.'

'Oh, I will.' *I will*. Wow, she didn't need an elevator, she was already floating.

But she left her stomach behind as the lift shot skyward. When the doors slid open again Jared was waiting in a matching robe. The warm golden glow of candlelight greeted her. Too many to count. Squat, thin, tall, a rainbow of colours, they were scattered over every available surface. 'Oh, my…Jared… this is…too much.'

'I told you before, there's never too much of a good thing.' He moved in for a long knee-weakening kiss. 'Mmm. You smell divine,' he murmured moments later.

'I *feel* divine.' She threw her arms around his neck. 'And my chakras are in perfect balance.'

'Are they now?' He sniffed her jaw. 'Jasmine?'

'And geranium and rose, with a whiff of citrus.' She licked his lips. 'Mmm. And you've been eating chocolate berries.'

'Strawberries, actually. Want one?'

'In a minute.' She lingered over the taste a moment longer, then moved to the wide panoramic window where a table held a bottle of celebratory bubbly and two glasses. Surfers Paradise nightlife sprawled below them like fairyland.

The view was as seductive as the man behind her. She caught his reflection in the darkened glass pane as he moved towards her. Tonight's whole experience was an aphrodisiac.

Watching his eyes in the glass, she poured two glasses of the wine but left them on the table and murmured a seductive, 'You know I'm naked under this robe.'

Large, firm hands reached out and squeezed her shoulders. 'I was counting on it,' he murmured back, his deep voice rumbling down her spine as he tugged the robe's belt open and drew the fabric off her shoulders. He kissed one shoulder then the other, pulled the robe completely away.

She heard the soft swish of air as he stripped off his own and then he turned her in his arms. He reached for the glasses, handed her one. 'To fantasies…whatever form they take.'

She raised her glass. 'To fantasies.' She took a sip. 'You've made mine come true, you know. I…I don't know how to…I can't—'

'Shh.' Jared put a finger against her lips. 'Not now.' He took their glasses, set them down on the table.

Jared didn't take his eyes off her as he carried her to the bed. This luxury suite might have been a dingy motel room on the edge of the Pacific Highway out of Ballina for all Jared knew, or even cared.

Their last night.

Their last time.

She rose up on her knees in the centre of the bed and he joined her, taking it slow as if they could make time stand still while the candlelight flickered and danced. Neither spoke but neither felt the necessity because everything was in their eyes as they watched each other. Their emotions, their desires, their awareness of the inverted hourglass.

They lay down together. It was different tonight. He felt it in the way she touched him, as if memorising the imprint of his skin against hers.

He was making his own memories. His lips lingered at her neck so he might recall the taste of her skin tomorrow, when she was gone. A week from now. A year.

He moved on top of her and, bracing himself on his elbows, stared down. Hair an ebony fan on the pillow, her own unique scent beneath the jasmine…just a shimmer of it in the air. Her eyes drenched with passion…and more.

Through fighting it, he almost surrendered to the inevitable. Was this the time to tell her that his feelings for her went deeper than they had for any woman he'd known? To ask her to consider something on a more permanent basis? Or tell her he'd meet her in a month for a weekend of loving in Paris before bringing her home to live with him.

He leaned down and kissed her. She moaned and moved beneath him as he slid inside her, her hands caressing his cheeks. Perhaps this was where she might tell him she'd changed her mind about going. Or that she'd be back in a month because she couldn't stand to be without him. She might ask him to take a break from work, to fly over and meet her for a romantic weekend in Paris or Rome, then surprise him by accompanying him back to Australia. To his bed, his home, his life.

And that would be the emotion of the night talking. But in the clear light of day…

Sophie's hands were cold. It was a clear Gold Coast day but she clamped them together to ease the chill while she waited beside her luggage. Her gaze roamed over the apartment she'd called home for the past four years. The plumped cushions, the cheery mugs on the kitchen bench. The first place she'd ever felt comfortable in. Safe in. Melissa would love it. Jared would no doubt come by and check on his sister…*Jared*.

Last night… Two fat tears welled up and spilled down her cheeks. When she was ready, when she was strong enough, brave enough, she'd write it all down. The man, the memories. She'd start a book of memoirs instead of a dream diary—she didn't need that crutch any more. Jared had taught her self-acceptance, given her back her self-esteem.

She just couldn't be the woman he needed.

He'd dropped her off after a quick lunch in the hotel's bistro and was coming by any moment now to take her to the airport. But he wouldn't be taking her—she'd booked a cab. No lingering farewells. A swift clean break.

She jumped at his familiar knock, checked her watch

then, inhaling a deep breath, walked to the door and pulled it open.

Their eyes met. The way they had the first time he'd come to her door. Same heart-stopping response. He'd always be *it* for her. She dredged up a smile. 'You're early.'

He didn't smile back, just stood there a moment, then rubbed a hand over his jaw. 'I wanted to talk to you before we leave for the airport.'

He closed the door, tangled her fingers with his to lead her to the couch. 'It might be easier if we sit down.'

Perched on the edge, she watched his eyes change, the way they did when he was deep in thought. Or deep inside her…

Her whole body went rigid—with fear, with hope, with fear again. Her heart wept in her chest. She would have clenched her fingers together again or pulled them away but he had a firm hold on both hands. She shook her head. 'I think we—'

'Sophie.' He looked down at their joined hands, then up to her eyes again. 'I realise my timing's all wrong, and maybe you don't want to hear this, but I can't let you leave without telling you.'

Her breath hitched and he paused, just looking at her like… like…

'I know you need to tick this trip off your list of life's goals,' he said, 'and if you don't you'll regret it. I will never intentionally tread on your dreams, Sophie, or try to stifle your life in any way, but I was thinking, *hoping*, that we might—'

'Stop.' She tugged her hands from his and pushed at him. 'Wait.' He was heading in a direction she couldn't go and her heart was already breaking. 'I need to tell *you* something first.'

Needing distance and at least some modicum of control, she stood. Not wanting to read what she'd see in those jade-green eyes, she needed to look somewhere else, anywhere but at his face. She dropped her chin, stared at the floor. 'I can't have children, Jared.' Her words choked in her throat and in the stunned silence she heard his indrawn breath. 'So whatever you were about to say, don't.'

She was aware of the muted traffic hum and small bird chatter outside the window. The refrigerator's noisy drone kicked in.

'Sophie…honey…' he began, finally. 'I…'

Closing her eyes, she shook her head. 'No. I don't want to hear it.'

'Okay. I need a minute here.' His voice was tight, as if he was having trouble breathing.

She knew. He was having trouble breathing because he was *deciding on the best way to extricate himself from the knot he'd been about to tie around his own throat.*

'I should have told you.' She opened her eyes, this time daring to look up, past compressed lips and into that maelstrom in his eyes. *Or maybe I shouldn't have told you at all.*

And now to tell him the whole truth and nothing but the truth. 'I fell in love with you, Jared. Your loyalty, your sense of humour, your perceptiveness, your integrity. You've given me the most precious of gifts. You valued me as an employee, desired me as a lover, you respect me as a woman. You've given me strength and a new belief in myself, but I can't give you what you want most.'

Jared stared at her while an iron fist pummelled his chest. 'Let me be the judge of that.' His words slashed the air, harsh and deep, like the shock carving a canyon through his body. 'I'll be the one who decides what I want.'

'Don't you see?' she said softly. 'I'm saving you from having to make that decision.' The sound of a car's horn drew her attention to the window. 'I have to go—I have a cab waiting.'

'But…hang on just a damn minute here.' He crossed to her in quick strides, caught her arm. 'I'm taking you to the airport. We arranged it.'

Again she lifted her hand to his chest. 'No. Please, no. I hate emotional airport goodbyes. It's better this way.'

'So you're…what…just dropping this bomb on me and leaving? Without giving me a chance to discuss this with you?'

'There's nothing to say. It's just the way it is.'

'The *hell* it is.' He slammed a fist against his thigh. He felt as if he were sinking in quicksand. He needed time but he didn't have it.

The buzzer sounded and she walked to the door, opened it. 'Good afternoon, just these cases,' she told the cabbie, indicating the two rolling suitcases beside her.

She swung a large bag over her shoulder, then placed her key on the kitchen bench. 'You'll need this to lock up.'

So caught up in the whirlwind tearing through his mind, he almost forgot, withdrawing a brown-paper package from his jacket pocket. 'Parting gift. Don't open it till you're on your way tomorrow.' He crossed the few steps between them, tucked it into her carry-all.

'Oh…thank you…' Her eyes welled with moisture. 'I left something for you too. With Melissa. She's at home with it, waiting for you right now.' She leaned close and whispered, 'Goodbye, Jared,' then kissed him softly.

Her lips clung to his for the longest time. Not long enough. Not nearly long enough.

And then she was gone.

A short time later he was staring down at the skinny black and white dog in Melissa's arms, a new red collar around his scrawny neck. 'What's the mutt doing here?' he demanded. But he couldn't resist scratching behind the silky ears. He'd always been a sucker where animals were concerned. 'Looks like he could do with a good feed.'

'This is Angus and he's from the pound. He's a year old so you don't have to worry about the puppy thing. He's fully house-trained and vaccinated and needs a loving home.' She held him out. 'He's yours.'

'Mine? I don't want a dog. What would I do with a dog?'

'He's Sophie's gift to you,' she said softly.

He frowned, stepping away, denying the choked feeling clawing up his throat. She'd given him a dog. 'What in hell was she thinking?' he muttered. 'You need to spend time with them, walk them, train them.' *Love them.*

That was what she'd been thinking.

'Sophie's thoughts exactly,' Lissa said. 'He'll be a companion now that you're on your own. You'll need to come home from work earlier—a good thing, Jared. Sophie understood that. She left food, bedding, toys…and a letter.'

He reached for the envelope in Lissa's hand.

Dear Jared,

Angus means 'unique choice', and that's what he is—the moment I saw him at the kennels, my search for a suitable companion for you was over. You said you didn't have time for pets but now you'll make the time. And in return, I promise that Angus will give you absolute loyalty and unconditional love.

Sophie.

CHAPTER FIFTEEN

BARELY over her jet lag, Sophie walked into a job in a London pub on her fourth day. Waiting tables wasn't her preferred choice but the position included meals and dormitory-style accommodation and it suited her fine for now.

It kept her hands busy and her mind occupied, she reminded herself three weeks later as she climbed the narrow staircase to the room she shared with two Aussies and an American from Philadelphia. Dwelling on Jared and what she'd left behind was a waste of energy and was a downer on what was supposed to be the best year of her life.

While she showered she reminded herself that even if he'd asked her to cancel her plans and stay with him she'd have said no. Which he wouldn't have, she thought, remembering his promise not to tread on her dreams. It was finally her turn and she'd worked long and hard for it.

Under different circumstances she might have told the man she loved she'd come back and asked him if he'd wait. But these weren't ordinary circumstances and this was no ordinary man. This was Jared, who loved kids, wanted a family and had already broken up with one woman because she didn't want children cluttering up their lives. In fact he'd been openly frank about it.

Her room mates had gone clubbing after their shifts but she'd told them she was too tired. She slipped into long flannel pants and a T-shirt and climbed into bed. It had become a nightly ritual to deal with her emails first. Another to tell herself she didn't expect Jared to contact her. And he didn't.

But every night she got that same fluttering anticipation in her belly when she opened her inbox, and the same dragging sensation when she didn't see his name. She'd had a couple of emails from Pam, but nothing about the office and Jared and how he was doing. Same with his sister. Melissa loved her new living arrangements, Angus was putting on weight and growing more handsome by the day. But no mention of his new owner.

Tonight was no different and she closed her laptop refusing to be disappointed. She was going to compose another entry in her new book of dreams instead. She caressed the silk-brocade-covered notebook. Jared's farewell package. He'd written on the first page:

Sophie,
For your dreams. May they all come true.
Always, Jared.

She'd spent the long-haul flight crying and staring out of the window and wondering what he was doing. What *she* was doing.

She'd unwrapped it somewhere over China and could almost hear him tell her, 'They'll be safer on paper...' And she could still see him smile that sexy smile that said he shared the joke.

Except now she wrote daydreams. Castles-in-the-air dreams. Where she and Jared and their offspring played happy families for ever after.

Impossible dreams that could never come true.

'Pam,' Jared boomed from his office at four o'clock one afternoon. 'The reports on those soil samples for Surfers' Retreat and Spa should've been back Monday. Get on the phone and give them a blast, I—'

'Calm down.' Pam popped her head into Jared's office and added in a lower but no less aggravated voice, 'You're frightening Mimi, not to mention little Angus there.'

He looked down at the bundle of black and white fur in the basket. Angus whimpered while two black eyes stared up at him. He didn't approve of dogs in the office, but this afternoon it had been unavoidable.

'It's okay, boy. Go back to your puppy-dog dreams. Liss'll be here to pick you up any minute now.' And didn't the mutt look spiffy with his new doggy trim and shampoo?

Shaking her head, Pam watched him like an exasperated parent complaining over her unruly child. 'I left a hard copy on your desk on Monday afternoon.'

Jared ran his hands down his cheeks and muttered, 'Where the hell is it now, then?' When Pam popped back out again, he muttered some more choice phrases she wouldn't want to hear.

He stared at his desk. Or what he could see of it. He'd sort it tonight when Pam went home. It would give him something to do. He leaned back in his chair and scowled.

Maybe he wouldn't sort it at all. He should take Angus for a walk on the beach. He'd left the little guy with Melissa too many times to count and it wasn't fair on the dog. Or Liss—she wasn't supposed to have pets in her apartment and was growing tired of splitting her time between her new home and his.

Sophie's idea wasn't working.

Sophie.

It had been over three weeks since she'd left. Three fiercely frustrating weeks where he lay in bed at night and remembered how Sophie had looked on their last evening together. How she'd felt beside him—smooth and sexy and silky.

Three long lean weeks where he didn't sleep, couldn't eat. Where he clocked up a ridiculous number of hours in the office and still his workload increased—no surprise there because his efficiency was decreasing.

He yanked open the filing cabinet beside his desk. Maybe he'd filed that report himself without reading it. Nope. He slammed the drawer shut again.

Sophie.

She'd smelled like summer and he found himself breathing deeply, as if he might conjure up the fragrance.

He hadn't contacted her but he knew she'd arrived safely because Pam had informed him. That had been a damn difficult day. It could only get better, right?

Wrong.

She'd left him. *Them.* There wasn't a *them*, he reminded himself. He'd had his chance to tell her how he felt. Days. Weeks, even. He'd always known she was leaving, she'd always been open about her plans.

She'd been honest about everything, except, it seemed, what mattered most.

She loved him.

She'd told him she loved him in the same breath she'd told him she couldn't have children. His silence had hurt her, he knew. But how was a man supposed to get his head around that bomb two minutes before she left for the other side of the world?

His open palm connected solidly with his desk. The registered packet that he'd signed for earlier today slipped a bit and caught his eye. He reached for it. The compact book slid out, he flipped to the first page and studied his photo. He'd never had a passport. Never needed one.

Pam appeared in the doorway and she didn't look happy. 'Impeccable timing,' he told her, leaning back in his chair, hands braced on the edge of his desk. 'Shut the door, I want to talk to you.'

'Good, because I have a few things to say to you too.' In a firm but businesslike manner she closed the door and sat down opposite him. Shoved a hand through her unruly brown locks. 'Does the word "resignation" mean anything to you?'

He barked out a humourless laugh. Then stared at her. She hadn't moved. Her mouth was flat, her eyes steady on his. 'You're serious.' Straightening, he rolled his chair nearer and placed his hands on the desk.

'Maybe I am. If you don't sort yourself out, I won't be the only one requesting that form.'

A strange feeling slid through him and his heart thumped hard in his chest.

'Excuses, stalling, evading,' she went on. 'They've never cut it with you, Jared, and they won't cut it with me. You're my friend as well as my boss, and Sophie's as close as a sister.'

She ran out of breath but he was the one who sat back as if he'd just run a marathon. He slid the legal document across the desk. 'So what do you say to this, then? How would you like to try out the boss's chair for a while?'

She met his eyes. 'Fine by me, but I'll need a raise.'

'You got it.'

She nodded, a smile chasing away the worry lines. 'That's the Jared I know.' Rising, she kissed him on the cheek and closed the door softly behind her on her way out.

He sat there and made lists, contacted clients, postponed projects while the sky turned from blue to apricot rose to aqua. He was still there when lavender had long turned indigo and a shimmering gold staircase on the sea pointed the way to a full moon rising.

Then he picked up the phone and called Liss. 'I know it's an imposition but I was wondering if you could stay over at the house for a bit and look after Angus. I'm taking a trip.'

When Sophie clicked into her inbox after her late shift a couple of nights later she saw the email she'd hoped for, waited for, dreaded. Her hands stilled on the keyboard, her breath hitched and everything, everything seemed to stop. Why now after all these weeks?

She blinked to make sure she hadn't imagined it, but there it was. 'Jared Sanderson' in bold black print. Flagged as high priority with a document with the enigmatic title of 'rustymagpie' attached.

Torn between elation and despair, she chewed on her lip while one finger trembled above the delete key. She could kill it with one click of a button. Any contact would jab at the still-raw wound in her heart and set her back by weeks.

Just this unopened email had the power to hurt simply by its very existence. Because she loved him and she'd opened her heart and told him everything and he'd rejected her. It could only be rejection, because he'd made no attempt to contact her. Nor did she expect him to. She'd not been honest with him until too late. She'd wanted him close as long as she could have him. Selfish. Thoughtless. No better than Bianca.

But like a chocoholic craving her next double-dipped dark-chocolate rum truffle, she clicked on his name. There was no message in the body of the email. She opened the attachment.

A rainbow of watercolours bled onto the screen as the file loaded. There was music, soft and sweet and low, a song about Sophie's presence still lingering there and not leaving him alone...

She knuckled moisture away from her eyes. Oh, he sure knew how to make her tear up. She should have deleted it. And yet...and yet...why would he do this?

The music finished and words scrolled onto the screen in a romantically flowing script:

Last night I had a dream. It was Tuesday morning. Ten o'clock—I remember because somewhere I heard a clock chime the hour. And I was standing at the Victoria Memorial in front of Buckingham Palace. Waiting for you. Charcoal clouds sagged, their underbellies like Spanish moss above the sculptured marble statues and Victory's gold wings. But still it was a magical place, just like you said.

And I made a wish. And in the way of dreams, the clouds dissolved and then the whole world was shining and golden and I turned and you were walking towards me with such a smile that I could barely breathe...

Sophie's breath caught. Now she was the one who could barely breathe. She concentrated on drawing air in, filling her lungs as far as she could. Letting it out slowly.

Tomorrow was Tuesday...

The realisation smacked her upright. No. No, no, no. She slammed the machine shut. Slid it to the bottom of her bed. *Not* possible. Jared was *not* in London and he was definitely *not* going to be waiting for her in front of the Victoria Memorial tomorrow morning. Never gonna happen. Lies. All lies, designed to make her...what?

She wanted to cry and scream and pull her hair out. *And dare to hope?* The best she could do was to drag the thin quilt over her head and pretend she'd never read it.

But of course she couldn't sleep. And she couldn't pretend. She sniffed under the cover of darkness and tried to sift through her jumbled thoughts and emotions. At ten o'clock tomorrow morning she was going to make sure she was sightseeing at Windsor Castle or Oxford or somewhere well away from Buckingham Palace.

Except...that was the coward's way out and if he really was here...he was here to see her...and what was that telling her? Had he really left his business and come all this way around the world *just to see her*?

You didn't come all the way around the world just to *see* someone. Her heart throbbed harder. Not ordinary people anyway.

Maybe it was just an email after all. To tell her…what…? Little shivers rippled up and down her body. What if…?

Jared stopped pacing a groove around the Victoria Memorial to check his watch for the third time in two minutes. If she didn't turn up soon he was going to wear a rut in the pavement.

He fisted his hands in the pockets of his coat. *Positive thoughts.* He was a positive kind of guy, wasn't he? Tourists swirled around him, snapping photos, enjoying London's brisk morning. It smelled of autumn and fresh-turned earth from the garden beds nearby. A couple of kids chased up and down the shallow steps.

Had she even read his email? he wondered for the millionth time. Maybe she didn't check daily… Maybe she hadn't understood the message.

Maybe she'd simply deleted it unread.

She'd be here.

And as if those words had conjured her up, there she was. Walking towards the memorial, her hands in the pockets of a rust-coloured coat. She wore black boots and a cream beret on her dark hair. Looking at her was like looking at a cream cupcake when you've been on a life-long diet.

When she passed the Buckingham Palace gates she caught sight of him and their gazes collided. Fused. He had to breathe in deep because suddenly he'd forgotten how. She appeared to falter, then picked up the pace again. Moving swiftly.

He moved too, dodging a group of noisy schoolkids on an excursion and for a moment he lost sight of her behind a tall robust man but then, there she was, smiling at him and he could smell her familiar fragrance before he could reach out and cup her face between his hands and lose himself in those dewy amber eyes.

He hauled her face to his before she could answer and kissed her. Tasted her unique sweet caramel flavour, heard her murmured sigh against his mouth. And all he knew was that he never wanted to let her go again. He drew back a little to see her better, stroking her cheeks before he took her hands and held them against his chest.

'Jared.' A shadowed expression crossed her face and her smile faded a little and he knew he'd put those shadows there.

'How long have you been here?' she asked, obviously expecting him to loosen her hands. 'In London, I mean.'

He didn't let her go. 'Just over twenty-four hours.'

'I got your email...' With a rueful grimace, she shook her head. 'Of course I did or I wouldn't be here...'

An awkward silence suddenly enveloped them. 'Let's go somewhere nearby where we can talk,' he suggested.

'St James's Park,' she said, indicating the way. Already a local, he thought, and, still holding one trembling hand, he accompanied her along the footpath.

They had a somewhat stilted conversation while they walked along Pall Mall. Her job was busy, she loved London. She'd seen the Tower and Westminster Abbey and been to Brighton on her day off last week. Melissa was enjoying her new apartment but staying at the house to babysit Angus. And yes, the mutt was gaining weight. A real personality, no doubt about that.

But all he could think was how right her hand felt in his, how he'd missed her, how much he wanted her in his life.

They passed through some beautiful ornate gates and, because the ground was damp, chose a wooden bench facing the lake. Autumn was busy here, painting a glorious palette of red and brown and gold amongst the green. A weeping willow on the little island in the lake reflected in the water. Even the air smelled different.

Sophie breathed in the scents of autumn and Jared. As long as she lived, she'd never forget this moment. They sat at an angle facing one another. He'd lost a few kilos. Fatigue shadowed his green eyes but there was emotion there too. And nerves, she thought, like her. She waited for him to speak first.

'Sophie.' He paused, then took both her hands and looked into her eyes. 'First off, I love you, Sophie. I'll always love you.'

She blinked up at him. Just for a moment her heart glowed and the whole world glowed with the wonder of it. A huge ball of emotion lodged in her throat.

'And knowing that you feel the same way, I have a question. The most important question I'll ever ask. Sophie Buchanan... will you marry me?' He squeezed her hands, his green-eyed gaze so tender and true she felt as if she'd been sliced through the heart, because it couldn't happen—not with them. She'd told him why.

'No.'

Something flitted across his gaze but he jogged their joined hands gently on his knees just once. Then he leaned in, pressed a quick but tender kiss on her lips. 'You told me you loved me—have you changed your mind already?'

'I... No.'

'Well, I sure as hell can't think of a single solitary reason why two people who love each other shouldn't get married.'

'You know why. Kids, Jared. You want kids. You...you told me you broke up with Bianca because she didn't want children.'

'Ah, Sophie, Sophie, is that what you thought?' He shook his head, pressed a kiss to her brow. 'I broke up with Bianca because she didn't want *Melissa* as part of the marriage deal. She expected me to shunt her off to her big sister after we got married and I wouldn't do it. That's entirely different, honey.'

'Oh...' It was, it was. Sophie's heart started to gallop.

'Now, is there any other reason?' he said. 'Because if there's not I'm going to ask you to marry me again.'

'You didn't try to stop me leaving, you didn't tell me you loved me when I left.'

'Because I was fighting my feelings. Afraid of how I felt. And I knew how much you wanted this trip, Sophie. I wouldn't dream of trying to stop you. After what you told me I needed time to think. I asked myself if I wanted those kids without you, and the answer is no. Never. You are my life, Sophie.'

She could no longer hold those carefully banked tears back and they spilled over and down her cheeks. 'I know how much you love kids, what a great father you'd make...'

Barely a pause, hardly a flicker in his eye. But there was something steely in the determined jut of his jaw. 'Sophie. *We* can't have children. We, plural. Shared. The two of us. Together. I'll say it again—*we* can't have children.'

Her tears spilled faster. He'd known, yet still he'd come all the way across the world for her. Because he loved her. He wanted to marry her.

'Tell me about it,' he begged her softly. 'Did you lose a baby? Is that why you didn't want anything to do with Arabella?'

She sniffed away her tears. 'I'd always wanted children. Glen wanted children almost as badly as me. But I'd always had problems in that area. When I didn't fall pregnant they ran tests. The doctors told me it was unlikely I'd ever conceive even with surgery, I had too much scarred tissue. And I was only twenty-one.

'Then a miracle happened. I was pregnant.' She looked down at her hands, remembering the heartache. 'It was an ectopic pregnancy. After...I only had one tube left and my chances were halved. Practically zero.'

She was conscious of Jared's hand over hers, his quiet empathy. 'Go on,' he murmured.

'Glen didn't see why he should miss out on being a father just because I was only half a woman—'

'Hang on, *half a woman*? He said that?'

She nodded and felt a tremor run from his hand to hers. 'So he set out to find a woman who could give him what I couldn't. He didn't consider being married to me to be an impediment.

Apparently he worked his way through quite a few lovers before he hit the jackpot.'

'Bastard.' The word slid out between clenched teeth.

'I think so.'

'Did you look at other alternatives? IVF, for instance?'

She shook her head. 'Why would Glen want to pay all that money with no guarantees? A divorce is faster and cheaper. And far easier to go out and find someone more fertile to father his offspring.'

'I'm not like Glen.' He seemed to choke on the man's name.

She looked into his eyes. 'I know you're not like him. But I've seen you with Arabella and I know how good you are with babies. You'd want your own children...'

He shook his head. 'Sophie, maybe under present circumstances we can't have our own children, but we haven't really given it a go yet, have we? You talked about your miracle—what makes you think two miracles can't happen? In the meantime we can look into those alternatives. And if all else fails, we can foster or adopt. There are always kids in need of loving homes. You have to remember, you're not alone in this. We're a team. All you have to do is say you'll marry me.'

'You mean that.' She breathed the wonder of it. 'You really mean it.'

'Don't look so surprised, honey.' Smiling at her, he stroked her hair. 'Of course I do, with all my heart and soul and everything that I have.'

'I love you too, and I don't want to be without you but it's taken me years to get here...I...haven't finished yet.'

'That's okay. I've taken leave. I've never taken leave so I reckon I deserve it. And I've got a nice suite for the two of us in a top hotel with a view of the Thames a ten-minute walk from your place of work. That is if you still want to work... Or would you rather travel the UK and Europe in style? With me.'

'Oh…' A whole new world was opening up to her. A world with Jared by her side…

'You don't have to be alone any more, Sophie. Let me be a part of your decisions. Let's make those plans together. Paris, Rome, Florence…wherever you want to go. As long as we go home together when we're done.'

Home. And she realised that was what she wanted, more than anything. To have this man—the man she loved—sharing her life. The good times…and the bad. She could still maintain her independence. She knew Jared would support her one hundred per cent in whatever she chose to do.

She looked up into his eyes warm with love. 'Yes,' she murmured, then louder, clearer, firmer, 'Yes. I'll marry you.'

The visitors to St James's Park might have looked on in amusement as he let out a joyous whoop then rose, hauling her up with him. 'Right answer,' he murmured, before laying his mouth against hers. Then, lips locked, he managed to twirl her around three times before setting her down.

He grabbed her hand once more and they began retracing their steps back to the Mall. 'Do you think you can get the evening off?'

'We have the afternoon…'

EPILOGUE

Two years later

SOPHIE smiled as she glanced out of the kitchen window while she stirred the gravy for their traditional lamb roast dinner. She loved lazy Sunday afternoons when all the family was here. Lissa and Jared were playing ball with a chubby little Arabella and a much larger Goldie while Angus chased and barked joyously between their feet. Crystal and Ian watched on under the shade of an umbrella.

They'd been back in Australia for twenty-two months now. It hadn't taken Sophie long to decide to give up the job in favour of being with Jared. They'd completed a whirlwind tour of the UK, France and Italy but in the end they'd just wanted to get home and become husband and wife and Jared couldn't neglect his business commitments any longer.

They were living in a beautifully renovated house with a large garden where Arabella could play when she visited, which was at least twice a week. Jared had given up his idea of condo living in favour of a more family-friendly home. Space to grow…

And miracles did happen twice. It had taken time, pain and a few disappointments, but now…Sophie touched her slightly rounded belly as she watched Jared pick up his squealing niece and toss her into the air. The modern miracle of IVF had given her a second chance. Given *them* a second chance.

At that moment Jared glanced at the window and she waved.

She saw him set Arabella down by Lissa and walk towards the back door. Twenty seconds later he was right there behind her, their linked hands resting over their unborn child. Already sixteen weeks along and everything was fine.

Sophie had never felt healthier in her life.

'What say we tell them the good news now?' he murmured against her ear. 'I don't think I can wait till after lunch.'

'Me neither.' She smiled. She was doing a lot of that these days. She checked the oven, untied her apron. 'Let's get this celebration started.'

He took her hands and lifted them to his lips, murmuring, 'Have I told you today how much I love you?'

'In so many ways,' she murmured back, kissing their joined hands.

And together they walked out into the sunshine.

Coming Next Month

from **Harlequin Presents®**. Available July 26, 2011.

#3005 THE MARRIAGE BETRAYAL
Lynne Graham
The Volakis Vow

#3006 THE DISGRACED PLAYBOY
Caitlin Crews
The Notorious Wolfes

#3007 A DARK SICILIAN SECRET
Jane Porter

#3008 THE MATCHMAKER BRIDE
Kate Hewitt
The Powerful and the Pure

#3009 THE UNTAMED ARGENTINEAN
Susan Stephens

#3010 PRINCE OF SCANDAL
Annie West

Coming Next Month

from **Harlequin Presents® EXTRA**. Available August 9, 2011.

#161 REPUTATION IN TATTERS
Maggie Cox
Rescued by the Rich Man

#162 THE IMPOVERISHED PRINCESS
Robyn Donald
Rescued by the Rich Man

#163 THE MAN SHE LOVES TO HATE
Kelly Hunter
Dirty Filthy Money

#164 THE PRIVILEGED AND THE DAMNED
Kimberly Lang
Dirty Filthy Money

Visit www.HarlequinInsideRomance.com
for more information on upcoming titles!

REQUEST YOUR FREE BOOKS!

2 FREE NOVELS PLUS
2 FREE GIFTS!

YES! Please send me 2 FREE Harlequin Presents® novels and my 2 FREE gifts (gifts are worth about $10). After receiving them, if I don't wish to receive any more books, I can return the shipping statement marked "cancel." If I don't cancel, I will receive 6 brand-new novels every month and be billed just $4.05 per book in the U.S. or $4.74 per book in Canada. That's a saving of at least 15% off the cover price! It's quite a bargain! Shipping and handling is just 50¢ per book in the U.S. and 75¢ per book in Canada.* I understand that accepting the 2 free books and gifts places me under no obligation to buy anything. I can always return a shipment and cancel at any time. Even if I never buy another book, the two free books and gifts are mine to keep forever.

106/306 HDN FC55

Name _____ (PLEASE PRINT)

Address _____ Apt. #

City _____ State/Prov. _____ Zip/Postal Code

Signature (if under 18, a parent or guardian must sign)

Mail to the **Reader Service:**
IN U.S.A.: P.O. Box 1867, Buffalo, NY 14240-1867
IN CANADA: P.O. Box 609, Fort Erie, Ontario L2A 5X3

Not valid for current subscribers to Harlequin Presents books.

**Are you a current subscriber to Harlequin Presents books
and want to receive the larger-print edition?
Call 1-800-873-8635 or visit www.ReaderService.com.**

* Terms and prices subject to change without notice. Prices do not include applicable taxes. Sales tax applicable in N.Y. Canadian residents will be charged applicable taxes. Offer not valid in Quebec. This offer is limited to one order per household. All orders subject to credit approval. Credit or debit balances in a customer's account(s) may be offset by any other outstanding balance owed by or to the customer. Please allow 4 to 6 weeks for delivery. Offer available while quantities last.

Your Privacy—The Reader Service is committed to protecting your privacy. Our Privacy Policy is available online at www.ReaderService.com or upon request from the Reader Service.

We make a portion of our mailing list available to reputable third parties that offer products we believe may interest you. If you prefer that we not exchange your name with third parties, or if you wish to clarify or modify your communication preferences, please visit us at www.ReaderService.com/consumerschoice or write to us at Reader Service Preference Service, P.O. Box 9062, Buffalo, NY 14269. Include your complete name and address.

HP11

Once bitten, twice shy. That's Gabby Wade's motto—
especially when it comes to Adamson men.
And the moment she meets Jon Adamson her theory
is confirmed. But with each encounter a little something
sparks between them, making her wonder if she's been
too hasty to dismiss this one!

Enjoy this sneak peek from ONE GOOD REASON
by Sarah Mayberry, available August 2011
from Harlequin® Superromance®.

Gabby Wade's heartbeat thumped in her ears as she marched to her office. She wanted to pretend it was because of her brisk pace returning from the file room, but she wasn't that good a liar.

Her heart was beating like a tom-tom because Jon Adamson had touched her. In a very male, very possessive way. She could still feel the heat of his big hand burning through the seat of her khakis as he'd steadied her on the ladder.

It had taken every ounce of self-control to tell him to unhand her. What she'd really wanted was to grab him by his shirt and, well, explore all those urges his touch had instantly brought to life.

While she might not like him, she was wise enough to understand that it wasn't always about liking the other person. Sometimes it was about pure animal attraction.

Refusing to think about it, she turned to work. When she'd typed in the wrong figures three times, Gabby admitted she was too tired and too distracted. Time to call it a day.

As she was leaving, she spied Jon at his workbench in the shop. His head was propped on his hand as he studied blueprints. It wasn't until she got closer that she saw his eyes were shut.

He looked oddly boyish. There was something innocent and unguarded in his expression. She felt a weakening in her resistance to him.

"Jon." She put her hand on his shoulder, intending to shake him awake. Instead, it rested there like a caress.

His eyes snapped open.

"You were asleep."

"No, I was, uh, visualizing something on this design." He gestured to the blueprint in front of him then rubbed his eyes.

That gesture dealt a bigger blow to her resistance. She realized it wasn't only animal attraction pulling them together. She took a step backward as if to get away from the knowledge.

She cleared her throat. "I'm heading off now."

He gave her a smile, and she could see his exhaustion.

"Yeah, I should, too." He stood and stretched. The hem of his T-shirt rose as he arched his back and she caught a flash of hard male belly. She looked away, but it was too late. Her mind had committed the image to permanent memory.

And suddenly she knew, for good or bad, she'd never look at Jon the same way again.

Find out what happens next in ONE GOOD REASON, available August 2011 from Harlequin® Superromance®!

Celebrating

Blaze **10** *years of*

red-hot reads

Featuring a special August author lineup of
six fan-favorite authors who have written
for Blaze™ from the beginning!

The Original Sexy Six:

Vicki Lewis Thompson

Tori Carrington

Kimberly Raye

Debbi Rawlins

Julie Leto

Jo Leigh

Pick up all six Blaze™
Special Collectors' Edition titles!

August 2011

USA TODAY *bestselling author*

Lynne Graham

introduces her new Epic Duet

THE VOLAKIS VOW
A marriage made of secrets...

Tally Spencer, an ordinary girl with no experience of
relationships... Sander Volakis, an impossibly rich and
handsome Greek entrepreneur. Sander is expecting to
love her and leave her, but for Tally this is love at first
sight. Little does he know that Tally is expecting his
baby...and blackmailing him to marry her!

PART ONE:
THE MARRIAGE BETRAYAL
Available August 2011

PART TWO:
BRIDE FOR REAL
Available September 2011

Available only from Harlequin Presents®.

www.Harlequin.com

HP13005